THE
KEY
PARTY

THE
KEY
PARTY

Lisa Nicole & Siddeequah

URBAN BOOKS
www.urbanbooks.net

This is a work of fiction. Any references or similarities to actual events, real people, living or dead, or real locals are intended to give the novel a sense of reality. Any similarity to other names, characters, places, and incidents is entirely coincidental.

URBAN SOUL is published by

Urban Books
10 Brennan Place
Deer Park, NY 11729

ISBN 1-59983-003-5

First Printing: July 2006
10   9   8   7   6   5   4   3   2   1

Printed in the United States of America

This book is dedicated to you, our readers.
We hope it invokes open-mindedness, teases your curiosities,
and captures your hearts!

Siddeeqah & Lisa Nicole

Acknowledgments

Special thanks goes out to Lisa Scott Hall and Marlo Jenkins for their insightful editorial skills. Many thanks to Ch-a, Lynn, Lakisha, Jazzy, Tony, Jacinth, Amy, Natasha, Thomas, Sheryl, Sandra, and Vivian for reading the book in its beginning and final stages and giving us the encouragement and the motivation to keep on writing. We would like to thank William Bell for his special contribution and our families and friends for their continued support, enthusiasm, and belief in us.

Thank you all very much,
Siddeeqah & Lisa Nicole

THE
KEY
PARTY

One

Dinner at Nikki's

"Is that the door?" Nikki said to herself. She dropped the knife and the carrot she had been slicing, wiped off her hands, and ran to answer it. It had to be Lynda. She was always early or right on time. Nikki was expecting everyone around seven-thirty. At least that's what the invitations said. It was seven o'clock now and she wasn't even close to being finished with dinner. Nikki got up on her tippytoes so she could look out the peephole to see who was there. She didn't see anyone and figured it was Lynda playing games. Nikki flung the door open and there was Lynda holding her invitation in front of her face. It had a gold key on the front of it.

Lynda and Nikki hugged each other tightly and then hurried back to the kitchen to get dinner finished up.

Lynda just loved Nikki's house. It had huge sixteen-foot vaulted ceilings, which made the rooms look larger. The main room was done in various shades of green and a nice neutral eggshell white. Nikki had hired an interior decorator to assist with the décor.

"So, Nikki, what the hell *is* a key party?"

Nikki was looking at Lynda over the top of her Chloé glasses. Lynda had always been very trendy. She was always dressed in an outfit you might see on one of those *E!* television shows. Always matching her purse with her shoes and accessorizing to no end. But that's what Nikki had always loved about Lynda. She looked good and she knew it! She didn't give a shit about what other people thought, either. Lynda was still waiting for Nikki's explanation.

"Lynda, let's wait for everyone to get here. I mean, that is the whole purpose of tonight's dinner. Everyone wants an answer to that question."

"Well, fix me a drink while I wait," Lynda said, rolling her eyes with her hands on her hips.

"What can I get you? I have some Woodbridge, Chardonnay, Sutter Home Merlot, and good old-fashioned liquor."

"Give me a Red Dog and quit playing with me, Nikki," Lynda said with a smile.

After Nikki handed Lynda her beer, the doorbell rang again.

"Hi, ladies," Nikki squealed as she opened the door and gave Kay and Renee each a big hug. Even though they had just seen each other earlier in the week, it was always great when the four of them got together. Kay had on some "bomb" red leather pants with a cute red cashmere sweater and red and black snakeskin boots. Renee, on the other hand, had her long black hair pulled back in a ponytail. She wore a pair of Gap jeans, brown cowboy boots, and a plain, white, short-sleeved T-shirt. Renee had always been able to pull off that plain, basic look and still look cute as hell! For twins, she and Kay sure dressed differently.

Since graduating from college, Nikki had made a special effort to plan a get-together for the four of them to get caught up. It was hard to stay as involved in each other's lives as they would like to, having responsibilities and lives of their own. Nikki had met Lynda her senior year in high school and they both met Kay and Renee the beginning of their sophomore year at Atlanta's Clark University. The twins were gorgeous and had come to Clark on a full track scholarship, moving from South Carolina to Atlanta to go to school. Lynda and Nikki were Atlanta natives.

Lynda was out of her seat and ready to give Kay and Renee some love by the time they all reached the kitchen.

"You ladies want something to drink while I'm up?"

"Yeah, Lynda, give me a vodka and cranberry please." Kay rolled her eyes at the sound of her friends mocking her for drinking the same damn drink since college. They were always messing with Kay; it was probably because she was "the big kid" in the group. She and Renee had just celebrated their twenty-eighth birthday days before. Nikki and Lynda turned thirty-one this past August.

"Let me have a glass of what you're sipping on, Lynda," Renee said.

Nikki had been drinking glass after glass of Chardonnay since five thirty and was starting to feel a little light on her feet.

"So where's Chris at, Nikki?" Renee and Kay said at the same time. They were always doing that, but Nikki and Lynda had gotten somewhat used to it over the years.

"You know Chris, he's at the office finishing up some work on a big project he's been working on. If he didn't have a male secretary I would swear he was cheating on me," she said jokingly.

"C'mon, Nikki, it's the year 2000. He and his secretary

could be tongue-kissing every chance they get, maybe even while Chris is calling home telling you he'll be late for dinner." Nikki looked over at Lynda, cracking up over her own joke.

"Ha . . . ha," Nikki said, giving Lynda the finger.

"So, Kay and Renee, what do you ladies think about this key party? Do you have any idea of what the hell it is? Because Nikki won't tell me shit until our men get here!"

"We have no idea," Kay said.

"We can't wait to hear what it's all about, though. We figure it's on the freak tip since Nikki put it together," Renee said.

"Oh, whatever," Nikki said loudly, "why I gotta be the freak? What about that time you and Kay did your little striptease for that guy you were dating? Sounds like some freaky shit to me!"

"Yeah, Nikki, but that was in college and it was on a dare so we did it. No big deal! It was harmless!"

Nikki had always thought of herself as more open-minded than most women. Even when she was in junior high and high school she went through phases where she questioned her own sexuality. She had been pretty shy throughout most of her teenage years and kept a pretty low profile as far as boys were concerned. She had always felt most comfortable with women.

At the beginning of her senior year of high school she had met Lynda, who changed her life forever. Lynda made her feel things she had never felt before. There was a confidence Lynda gave Nikki about herself that Nikki loved more than anything. Nikki felt invincible when she and Lynda were together. Lynda always lived life to the fullest, like she was the only one who mattered; not in a bad way, but in a way that let you know not to mess with her. She slowly helped Nikki to come out of her shell.

Lynda was extremely outgoing and was constantly being propositioned by guys. She even went to the senior prom with the captain of the football team, which was classic since she was cheerleading captain. His name was Rick and he really was a terrific guy. He was definitely a "keeper," as Lynda would always say! Nikki did end up getting asked to the prom by some arbitrary loser whose name she had tried to forget over the years. It ended up being a halfway decent time in the long run. Lynda lost her virginity to Rick and Nikki got felt up and had her first kiss with what's-his-name.

The next fall when Lynda and Nikki both got accepted to Clark University, Nikki was ecstatic; she couldn't have imagined college without Lynda. They had both grown up in Atlanta so they wouldn't be going far, but living on campus was going to make all the difference in the world. Their freshman year would turn out to be a huge learning experience for several reasons. One night following final exams, Nikki found answers to questions she had been asking herself for years.

She and Lynda had been chilling in Nikki's room getting ready to go out to this spot where all the football and basketball players hung out, called 112. They always drank their wine and blasted music while they walked around in their panties and bras getting ready for the night ahead. They had one too many drinks in celebration of finishing all of their final exams. Lynda was standing behind Nikki helping her pin her hair up and the next thing she knew she could feel Lynda's warm body pressed against her back. Lynda started kissing Nikki softly on the back of her neck. Nikki didn't

expect her panties to get as wet as they did as quickly as
they did. Lynda's tongue moved slowly along the bottom
of Nikki's jawbone, darting across the left side of her
neck. The kissing quickly progressed to sucking, to touching, and eventually they were both breathing pretty heavily, getting extremely turned on. Nikki didn't care at the
time that a woman was giving her pleasure beyond her
wildest dreams; she just enjoyed the moment while it
lasted. When Nikki turned around she was face-to-face
with Lynda. Reality hit and they both realized they were
out of control. They made an unspoken agreement that
night to forget what happened. Blame it on the liquor,
was the way the old saying went. Most of what happened
next would become blurry over the years. They broke
their pact a couple of times after that night. They shared
a couple more deep and even passionate kisses and had
both let their hands explore a bit.

That summer following their freshman year Lynda
and Nikki lost touch—for no particular reason that Nikki
could figure out. Nikki never thought it was directly related to the intimate moments she and Lynda had
shared; she felt that they simply just grew apart. Those
moments with Lynda had made Nikki realize that although she had always had a strong appreciation for
women, she was far from being a lesbian. She still knew
that men made her the happiest. Over time she and
Lynda met up again, reestablished a bond, and were
the best of friends to this day.

Chris had to finish up a status report for his boss and
then he was going to head downtown to meet Rick for
some racquetball. They had an old score to settle. His
job at Marketing Zone, Inc., was to help define a com-

pany's marketing strategy. He even got what they called "Thinking Days" off. On those days he was supposed to simply *think* and come up with good ideas for the account they were working on. The company had been good to him and he enjoyed the success he'd found there.

It would only be his second time on the court since tearing his ACL on a fluke while playing tennis a year ago. It was a really shitty experience for Chris and he'd been too nervous to play sports for a while; he just didn't want to risk injury again. He even brought his brace with him so he could put it on Rick real good. They only had about an hour to play, so Chris was trying to finish things up pretty quickly. He was going to try and beat Rick there, but he knew he wouldn't. Since Rick had married Lynda he was always on time. Lynda did not play about that shit!

Chris was shutting down his system and had his finger ready to shut his monitor off when the phone rang.

"Chris Reynolds."

"Hi, baby, it's me."

He could recognize Nikki's voice in a roomful of people all talking at the same time.

"Hi, sweetheart, what's up?"

"Can you please bring home two bottles of that Merlot I love? The girls are all here and we have finished two bottles already."

"Are you talking about that Ironstone Merlot? I hope so, because you suck a mean dick after you've had a couple of glasses of that stuff."

"Yup, that's the one!" Nikki said, chuckling. "And, baby, if you get here on time I might even hook you up in the bathroom while everyone is clearing the dishes away."

"Girl, let me go before you get me all excited. I'll be

there at eight with two bottles of Ironstone, one in each hand and a nice stiff dick in my pants."

"See you later, honey, and thanks again."

Chris had asked Nikki to marry him back in '92, but he remembered it as if it were yesterday. They had met at a PR firm where they both worked as interns in college. Chris thought Nikki was the most beautiful woman he'd ever seen the very first time that he saw her. They had dated for about two and a half years when he decided that Nikki was without a doubt the woman he wanted to grow old with. He bought the ring that she had been pointing out to him for quite some time. He wrote the check for seventy-five hundred dollars without batting an eye. It was a small price to pay for the girl he had been dreaming of all his life.

That night he took Nikki to her favorite restaurant, the Lobster Bar. They had a wonderful dinner followed by passionate, rough, and raunchy sex. Nikki had always been a freak and he loved that. After he knew she was fast asleep, he took the ring out of the box and slipped it on her finger. It looked perfect! The following morning he got up at five to make sure he would be out of the house way before Nikki woke up. He wrote a note and left it on her nightstand with the ring box sitting on top of it. The note was simple. It said, *While you were sleeping I asked you to marry me . . . when you awake I hope that you'll make my dream come true!*

He went to work and waited anxiously for the phone to ring. Instead, Nikki showed up at 7:00 a.m. with tears flowing from her big brown eyes. He cut out the lights in his office and closed the blinds and proceeded to make love to his future wife right there on the Persian rug of his office floor. At that moment, he was the happiest man alive.

* * *

When Chris snapped out of his daydream, he dashed out of his office, jumping into his forest-green Range Rover. He loved his truck! When he pulled up to the Peachtree Athletic Club he saw Rick's car out front, a 1999 navy blue Lexus LS. Chris had wanted one of those, but Nikki had one and they figured that the SUV made better sense since they wanted to start on a family in a year or two. Chris dropped his things in the locker room and saw Rick through the tiny glass window of the court doors. They always played on court number 4 as long as it was available. There was no particular reason, just one of those guy, sports things.

Chris opened the door, interrupting Rick's warm-up. Rick grabbed the ball and ran over to give Chris a high five. They got going on their first match and Chris was up by four points.

"So how is everything going?" Rick said, barely out of breath.

"Things are great, man. Work is going really well, we actually just got a real big account sealed up yesterday. With this one under my belt, that senior VP position should be mine in no time. Nikki and I are doing great too. The happier I keep her, the happier I seem to be. I learned that trick about a year ago. How about you and Lynda, man, is everything cool on the home front?"

"Yeah, we're real cool. Lynda has been able to double her client base over the last year or so and my construction company just signed a contract to build a new state-of-the-art high-rise apartment community in Buckhead. Things have been slow in the bedroom, though. I think Lynda's just been real tired, so I don't take it personal."

Yeah, right, Chris thought to himself. He had heard

from Nikki that Rick left much to be desired in the bedroom; at least that's what Lynda told her.

"I hear you, man," Chris said. "Don't sweat it too
tough. They're always going through something. You
just have to get it while the getting is good."

"Game point!" Rick yelled as he served it up to finish
their final match. Chris was hustling to get to the ball
until Rick smacked the hell out of it and ended the
game.

"Good game," Rick said with a smug-ass look on his
face. He had beaten Chris four games out of seven.

"Damn it! Oh well, next time, man . . . I'm gonna get
you next time." They showered, changed, and headed
to Chris's house.

It only took twenty minutes to get to Chris and
Nikki's place from Peachtree Street.

They had bought their house about a year and a half
ago after tiring of apartment life, wanting to own their
own home. Chris and Rick pulled up into the driveway
and grabbed the Merlot they had stopped to get on the
way in. They could hear the women laughing and chat-
ting all the way outside.

Kay and Renee were helping get the table set and
Lynda and Nikki were tying up loose ends in the kitchen.
Kevin, Kay's boyfriend, and Jason, Renee's fiancé, had
arrived minutes earlier and were chilling in the living
room watching the Knicks vs. Lakers game. Everyone
knew that Kevin was a *huge* Knicks fan mainly because
his favorite player, Allan Houston, was on the team.
Renee and Jason had gotten engaged about five months
ago and Kay and Kevin had been seeing each other for
a little over a year.

Chris and Rick came in and kissed all the ladies, then
hurried to the kitchen to grab beers. They both found

empty spots on the couch next to Kevin and Jason. The Knicks were up forty-five to thirty-three when Nikki called them all into the dining room to eat. All the guys came filing in, one behind the other, straining their necks to catch the last few seconds before halftime.

"Yeah!" Kevin yelled, jumping up and down and cheering. Allan had thrown a Hail Mary at the buzzer and made it.

"Well, fellas, now that we have your *undivided* attention, can we all please join hands and pray?" Nikki said. Everyone bowed their head to pray and then dug right in, reaching and passing dishes here and there. Like at all good dinner parties, for the first minute or so there was absolutely no conversation. The food was delicious and Nikki had to interrupt to get conversation going. She cleared her throat between bites and asked, "So, did everyone get their invitations?" Jason and Renee spoke up first, saying they left theirs at home. Kevin pulled his out of his pocket and threw it on the table.

"Kay and I have no idea what a key party is, but we're always down for the get-down. Right, baby?" Kevin said, winking in Kay's direction.

Kay smiled sweetly at Kevin; he was so much fun, she thought.

"The suspense of all this is killing me and Rick," Lynda said. "So let's hear it. What is a key party?"

Two

The Rules

Nikki took a deep breath and began to explain. "All right, here's the deal. A key party is usually held at someone's house or even in a hotel room because it's really just a prelude to the actual party. All of the women come to the party with their house key attached to a label or tag with their name and address on it. Each person should drive separately if possible. All of the women's keys are dropped in a bowl that stays near the front door. After that, we just party all night long like we normally would. The women leave about thirty minutes before the men and once the guys are ready to go, they just grab a key out of the bowl. The rest is pretty self-explanatory. What happens that night is between you and your partner in crime so to speak."

Nikki glanced over at Chris to see how he was taking all of this. He had the same embarrassed and appalled look that he had when she had initially introduced the idea to him. As Nikki finished talking, she realized that the room was completely silent and all eyes were on her.

Renee had dropped her fork at some point during Nikki's explanation and Kevin had a big Ronald McDonald grin on his face. Jason was looking at Renee in disbelief, wondering what kind of friends she had. Rick was looking at Lynda, his eyebrows raised, and Kay was looking at Nikki, shaking her head. Bottom line, no one was saying a word.

Nikki cleared her throat. "Okay, well, um . . . I'll give you all a second to process all that," and then she took her seat next to Chris.

Nikki knew at that instant what was going through everyone's mind. They were all thinking about the incident that had happened about nine months ago.

Nikki had planned a "let's get together for the hell of it" party. She invited the whole crew over to eat, drink, and just chill—enjoying each other's company. For some reason, she got the notion that it would be a good idea to take it back to the old school. You know . . . wayyyyyyyyyyy back. She went to the kitchen and brought back an empty bottle. She came back into the living room, holding it high in the air over her head.

"Spin the bottle, anyone?" Nikki said with a sneaky look in her eyes. People had been talking and laughing so loud that they hadn't heard her. Nikki stood up on the end of her teal-green leather couch and yelled, "*Spin the bottle, anyone?*" This part was funny to her because she remembered Chris having to jump up and save her from breaking her neck when she damn near fell off the arm of the sofa. Kevin stopped midsentence in the conversation he was having with Renee and looked up at Nikki.

"I'm down," Jason said, amazingly the first one to reply.

"I'm in," Lynda said, coming out of the kitchen into

the living room, taking a seat on the floor, sitting down Indian style.

"I'll play but no tongues," Kay said.

"Ditto," Renee said.

"That's cool," Rick said, "let's do it."

Chris just looked at Nikki in amazement; she always knew how to get everyone's juices flowing, *that* was for sure. By this time, everyone was sitting practically shoulder to shoulder waiting for Nikki to take her seat so they could begin.

"All right, people, this is the deal. You spin the bottle and whomever it lands on, you'll take them into the closet in the foyer straight ahead. You have to close the door and stay in long enough for us to count to five out loud. Please keep it simple and clean, no hits below the belt," Nikki joked. "The most important rule to remember is, *Keep your hands to yourself!*"

"I think we have the idea, Nikki," Renee said.

"This is a simple game, no harm, no foul. Who's the oldest here?" Nikki asked, staring dead at Lynda. Lynda yanked the bottle out of Nikki's hand.

"I'll start," she said, giving the bottle its first spin.

Lynda's spin landed dead center facing Rick. She tried to contain her disappointment. It wasn't that she didn't want to kiss Rick but, c'mon, he was her husband and that's not what the game was about. Lynda and Rick ran in and ran out. They were out before the group could even get to a count of five.

"All right, Rick, your turn," Nikki said. Rick spun the bottle and it landed on Jason.

"What are you guys looking at?" Jason said, looking around at the rest of the group. "I'm not that fucking drunk!" Everyone started laughing.

Rick stood up and yelled, "Rule number two. No

dudes kissing dudes. That's not what this brother is about."

"Just calm down, Rick," Chris said. "We know you've been hoping to get a chance with Jason." Everyone was cracking up and laughing at Rick.

"Ha, ha, hell," Rick said, sitting back down. "I get to spin again, right?" he asked.

"Yeah, go ahead, Rick," Nikki said.

Rick spun it again and this time it landed on Kay. Kevin instinctively turned to look at Rick. Kay hopped up and said, "C'mon, Rick, it will be over before you know it." They ran in there and stood silently for a second, but they could already hear the crew screaming, "Two . . . Three. . . ."

Fuck it! Rick thought, as he leaned in and touched Kay's soft glossy lips with his . . ."Five." It was over! *Wait,* Rick thought, *we're not, I mean, can we* . . . Kay had already grabbed his hand and was pulling him out of the closet.

Lynda hadn't seemed to mind the fact that her husband had just kissed another woman for the first time in ten years. Instead it was kind of exciting seeing him come out of the closet with another woman.

"Okay, I'm next," Nikki said. Lynda was checking out her cuticles, making sure her manicure was still tight. She wondered why everyone had grown so silent. When Lynda looked up she saw the bottle staring back at her.

"What now?" Renee said.

"Um, I guess it's up to the person that spun," Nikki said.

"It's just a quick kiss," Lynda said, standing up. They walked over to the closet and closed the door behind them. It had been a long time since their experiences in college, but at that moment it seemed as if it had happened yesterday. "One . . ." Nikki leaned over and gave Lynda a quick kiss on the lips. No sparks flew or anything to that effect for Nikki. But Lynda had confirmed one thing. She was still very attracted to Nikki. She always had been, and after that kiss she knew she always would be. "Five . . ." They opened the door and ran back to take their seats on the floor.

"All right," Nikki said. "Three more spins and we're moving on to some other scandal." Lynda spun the bottle, hoping to get Nikki again, but it landed on Chris. Chris hopped up and puffed his chest out.

"All right, Miss Lynda, let me show you what this is all about," he said, putting his arm around Lynda's neck, looking back at Rick and smiling. He was only kidding and he knew Rick was a good sport. They jumped in, looked at each other, gave a quick smooch, and came back out. Chris came out adjusting his belt, just to fuck with Rick.

"Keep on, man, and your ass will get kicked up in here," Rick said jokingly. Chris spun the bottle and it landed on Renee.

"There's just not enough of me to go around to all you ladies, so please try to control your spinning," Chris said.

"Whatever, let's get this over with," Renee said. She ran in and gave Chris a quick peck on the cheek. Chris felt cheated, but he wasn't going to argue the rules.

"Okay, people, last spin," Nikki said. Renee picked up the bottle and spun it. It seemed to go around forever before it finally stopped and was pointing directly at Kevin. Kay looked a little surprised. No big deal, she thought, she just wasn't expecting it, that's all. Renee and Kevin hopped up and walked the long walk to the closet. When they got inside it took a second for Kevin to realize what was about to happen. He had always wanted to do this.

"Okay," Renee said, "kiss me and let's get out of here." Kevin placed his arms around Renee's waist and pulled her close to him. He grabbed her face and softly parted her lips with his. Their tongues were in each other's mouths by the time they heard "Four!" He didn't want to stop. He could feel himself getting turned on. How could he walk out of the closet like this? He put his hand down Renee's pants and got no objection, much to his surprise. What did this mean? Kevin was asking himself. They weren't counting anymore outside and the silence was scary. Kevin wanted to run out the back of the closet and Renee wanted to dig a hole and bury herself in it.

"Okay," Renee said, whispering, "we'll just go out and pretend like we stayed in longer on purpose just to mess with Kay and Jason."

"Cool," Kevin said.

When they opened the door, you could hear the hinges rotating it was so quiet. All eyes were on them.

"We were just fucking with y'all," Kevin said, giving Jason "dap" and smiling that million-dollar smile of his. Kevin didn't realize that he had a hard-on the size of Montana clearly visible to everyone.

"*Game over*," Kay said, standing up. "Let's go before I go off up in here and embarrass both of us."

"What?" Kevin said. "It's just a game, Kay. Please sit down and let's just enjoy the rest of the night."

"Just a game, huh? It seems to me like you may need to go and take a cold shower before we do anything else."

Kevin looked down and was horrified to see that his

dick was rock-hard and had risen to the occasion. There was nothing he could say.

"Kay, nothing happened, you know how easily men get excited, I swe—"

"Shut the hell up," Kay said to Renee. "I don't want to hear shit from you for about a week."

"What did I do?" Renee said, rising to her feet. "I'm playing a damn game just like everyone else!"

"Yeah, Renee, you're never trying to hurt anyone, right? I'm out of here," Kay had said, getting up. "And, Nikki, next time you want to play one of your sex games, leave me out of it! Peace!"

Nikki knew it had taken the crew a long time to recover from that night, especially Kay. Eventually Kay forgave Renee and just chalked it up to Kevin being easily excited. Jason and Renee were able to forget about it and move forward. At least that's what Jason told Renee.

"I know you guys are thinking about the 'little' spin-the-bottle incident," Nikki said, interrupting everyone's flashbacks.

"We've all gotten past that, though, right?" Nikki said, unsure of her statement.

Everyone continued eating, but their minds were going a million miles a minute; they were all thinking something different. Kevin was thinking that this was his chance to have Renee the way he had always wanted her. Rick didn't feel strongly about it one way or the other; he just viewed it as a change of pace. Jason was just hoping that Renee wouldn't be down with this craziness. Chris was getting warmed up to the idea and was looking at the options that sat in front of him. Lynda was fine with it for the most part and so was Kay. Renee spoke first.

"I just think everyone needs some time to determine where he or she stands on the idea. As individuals and as couples. I mean, this could end up being catastrophic, don't you think, Nikki?"

"Only if you're thinking of it in catastrophic terms," Nikki said. "I do agree, though, that everyone should go home and give all of this some serious thought. Just let me know your decision in about a week and a half. That will be somewhere around the eighth. The party is going to be on October thirteenth. Now let's enjoy the rest of this evening without mentioning the words 'key' or 'party.' Hope to see your cards next week!"

Nikki took her seat with a wide smile on her face. For the first time since that night of playing spin the bottle, the group was looking at each other in another light. Considering that they could actually be experiencing each other in ways that were once thought to be unimaginable. For most of them, it was at least an exciting thought, but for Jason it was torturous.

Three

R.S.V.P.

Jason dropped Renee off at her door and gave her a kiss good night.

"Don't you want to at least come in so we can discuss this key-party thing together?" Renee said. "You haven't said two words the entire drive home."

"No, baby, I'm gonna go home and sort things out in my head a little bit first if you don't mind. We can talk about it tomorrow at dinner."

Thursday was their six-month engagement anniversary and Jason had made reservations at his favorite steak place, just for the two of them. He was so excited about the future they had planned together; he really loved Renee and wanted to make her as happy as she always made him. After the wedding they were going to get an apartment together, somewhere near downtown since they both worked in that area.

"All right, well, don't dwell on this thing," Renee told Jason. "If you don't want to do it, we don't have to, you know," she said reassuringly.

"I know, I just need a minute to clear my head. I love you," he said, giving her a kiss on the forehead. He stayed in front of the door until he could hear that she locked the door and pulled the chain across inside.

He drove for hours, finally stopping his car to get out when he reached Centennial Park in downtown Atlanta. He figured the evening fall air could probably do him some good. He had always loved the fall anyway, especially October. The chill in the air meant Christmastime was just around the corner; everyone was in good spirits and had the whole yuletide cheer thing going on. It was times like these when he really missed his family.

He had spent his early years growing up in Dayton, Ohio. His mom and dad had always been great to him and his sister, Jessica. He used to call her Jess for short. His parents had been married for twenty-eight years when his dad left his mom for another woman. A black woman. That wouldn't hold much importance if his dad wasn't black and his mom wasn't white. In this case, it was crushing to his mom and only added insult to injury in her mind. It had been unexpected and had destroyed the family completely. And that wasn't even the worst tragedy to strike Jason's happy home.

When he was nine, his older sister, Jessica, had been struck and killed by a drunk driver while walking home from school. His mother had never recovered and Jason suffered tremendously. He had always been an exceptional student and his parents were very supportive until Jess's accident. There had never been a time that he looked up in the middle of a tennis match or from his lane at one of his swim meets and didn't see his parents in the stands. He and his mom had been very close until his dad left; after that, it seemed that she just lost her motivation. She didn't have anything left. And as Jason started to become a man, she depended on him for companionship way beyond the normal call of duty. The first time it happened was a year to the day that his dad had packed the car up and left. Jason had come home from a movie with his best friend and their dates. His best friend's mom dropped Jason off at his house and he said good-bye to his little hanging buddies.

When he walked into the house he could hear the music playing loudly. It was Nat King Cole and she only played it when she would wake up and be in one of her dark moods thinking about his dad. Sometimes it would take her weeks to snap out of it. He took a deep breath and opened the door. She had been drinking all day. He could smell the Jack Daniel's from the door and then he saw his mom standing directly in front of him. Her nightgown was dirty from wearing it for a week straight. Her eyes were swollen and her face was puffy almost beyond recognition. She had been crying all day and was unsteady, standing in a drunken haze.

"Is that you, Steven?" she said.

"No, Mom, it's me. It's Jason." Jason knew why she was asking for Steven. That was his dad's name.

Jason walked over to his mom and took the newly poured drink out of her hand. He walked her over to the couch and helped her have a seat. She was crying uncontrollably.

"Why are you late?" she screamed. "You're cheating again, aren't you? Aren't you?"

Jason was crushed. He couldn't stand to see her like this. "Mom, it's me. It's Jason."

She looked confused and then reared back and slapped his face. He was stunned but realized she really thought it was her husband. He hugged his mom and held her close to him. She melted in his arms. She felt so fragile and vulnerable at that moment. He just wanted to save her from the demons of his sister's death and her failed marriage, the things that haunted her every single day.

"Are you okay, Mom?" he said, stroking her hair gently.

She looked up at him and said, "Make love to me, Steven, just one last time."

He couldn't take it anymore. How much longer would she expect him to play the role of his father who had deserted them? He pushed her away in disgust. She looked devastated. She ran over to him and started to kiss him, started to kiss her own son. She had already lost so much. How could he deny her too? He hated the sound of his belt buckle coming undone the most. The sound would haunt him later in life.

He laid her down on the couch and made love to his mother as best he could. He just did what he saw on the movies and what his minimal experimentation with his fifteen-year-old girlfriend had taught him. It always seemed to be enough for his mother either way. When he was finished, he tried to bury the filth and shame he felt by taking a hot shower. He wrapped his arms around himself and just hoped the hot water would somehow drown the misery of what his happy life had become. That night became a ritual for Jason, one he could never talk about with another soul. Even after both of his parents passed away, he would keep his secrets so as not to defame them and himself. After all, he was just being the obedient son, the one who had survived.

* * *

Jason woke up and realized he had been dreaming about his mom again. He had huge bags under his eyes to show for it. He got up and turned the shower on full blast. Even as a man the showers helped him to forget his painful past. He was in and out pretty quick and on his way to work. He knew he would have a message from Renee asking what had happened last night. For years he hadn't been able to perform sexually. It wasn't until he met Renee that he felt comfortable enough to let his guard down. Renee had been great about it all and he appreciated her patience with him. After all, he had always considered himself to be a work in progress.

The first time they made love had been about seven months after they had started dating. They had come home from the Fox Theatre's performance of *Phantom of the Opera*. Renee had been looking delicious to him all night. He even had a hard time keeping the erection from coming. When they got home he just couldn't resist her anymore. He told her he wanted to make love to her on the spot. Right there in the foyer, he got down on his knees and began to nuzzle her crotch with his nose like a puppy. He unzipped her pants and went to the fridge, coming back with a strawberry. He pushed it all the way inside her and then ate it out.

He stuck his entire face, it seemed, inside Renee. She was in ecstasy and he loved it. He was nibbling on all of her weak spots, bringing her to her knees literally. At that point, he couldn't wait anymore. He took off his pants and tried to block out the sound of his belt buckle coming undone. He made love to her on the foyer for what seemed like an eternity. He carried her into the bedroom and laid her on the bed under the covers. He whispered in her ear, telling her he loved her, and thanked her for a wonderful night. He then took a long shower and lay in bed next to her.

That had been an experience he had never forgotten. Since then, lovemaking had become a regular activity for the two of them and he had some special things planned for their engagement anniversary later that evening. The message on his voice mail at work sounded slightly frantic. Renee was concerned and wanted him to call her as soon as he made it to work. He decided he would call her after his 9:00 a.m. meeting was over. He was already running a little late. He grabbed his leather-bound notepad and Cross pen and headed toward the main conference room. He would consider the key-party idea while he daydreamed during his meeting.

I hope he's Okay, Renee thought. She hated when he went through these times and shut her out completely. It happened at least once a month and there was not much she could do to help. He just had to snap out of it himself. She knew he was struggling with some things that had happened to him growing up, but he had never gone into much detail. All she knew was that he was an only child and that both of his parents were deceased. He had some extended family that lived in Dayton, but he never really talked about them or went out of his way to keep in touch. She knew he took medicine for depression, just something to keep him from staying in the funk all the time. She had forgotten the name of it, but it didn't bother her that he needed it to help him get through each day. She knew he loved her, but **it** *was* difficult to be there for him during these times.

He had been working at Chambers & Chambers since his internship in college. After he finished law school, they had presented him with the opportunity to become a partner. He had been ecstatic; he was smart and really knew his shit. That was a huge turn-on for Renee. The relationship had been really good for both of them. They met at a time when they both really needed someone. Renee had just gotten out of a pretty rocky relationship and Jason was allowing himself to trust women for the first time.

He was unlike any other man Renee had ever dated. He was so conscious of the little things, which made a world of difference to her. Things like picking up Renee's dry-cleaning when she least expected it, or having lunch delivered to her office on days that he knew she would be too busy to eat. He always "took care" of her and it was so nice.

The first time he had one of his attacks was at a Thrashers game. It was extremely crowded and they couldn't find their seats. Renee noticed that he looked very uneasy and was getting more and more frustrated with the whole situation. She told him to relax and said that they would find the seats eventually, no big deal. He rolled his eyes and continued to look for their section. The crowd was even thicker near their aisle and that's when Jason came undone. He looked dazed and confused and had to lean on the wall to support himself. Renee didn't even notice that he had slumped all the way down to the ground until the woman behind her tapped her shoulder and pointed at Jason down on the ground holding his chest.

"What's wrong, baby?" Renee said, frantic as hell. "What's happening?"

"Nothing," he said, shooing her away. "Just give me a minute, okay? I just need one fucking minute."

He had never cursed at her before, so she knew that something was very wrong. "Do you need some water? Some wet paper towels or something?"

"No, baby, please just give me room to try and catch my breath. Actually, yeah, give me some water please." He pulled the vial out of his coat and held the two orange pills in his hand with a look of contempt and disgust on his face. Why couldn't he get his shit together? he thought to himself. Why did he have to be so weak all the time? The last thing he had wanted to do was to run Renee off.

When she came back, she saw him putting the medicine back in his coat pocket. She decided to fight the urge to ask about it until the ride home.

They left before the game started and on the way home Jason explained that he suffered from panic attacks from time to time. The medicine he took was called Xanax, an antianxiety drug. It helped him gain his composure when he couldn't do it himself. He didn't mention that he used to take Prozac, Zoloft, and finally Paxil years ago and that he had made strides to get to the point of *only* needing to take the Xanax to calm him down. Renee knew he was embarrassed and didn't want to make too big a deal out of things.

"I just wish you had told me, baby, so I would have known what was going on. I thought you were having a heart attack."

"I'm sorry," Jason said with a genuine heartfelt look in his eyes. "I just didn't want to freak you out."

"That's okay, we all have our demons, sweetheart."

She kissed his cheek, reassuring him that there was nothing he couldn't share with her. One day she hoped he would be comfortable enough to share more of the things that tore him up inside.

Renee came back to the present just in time to hear the phone ring. It was Jason telling her that he was okay and that he had just gotten out of his Monday morning meeting. He wished her a happy anniversary, which made her smile. "You too, sweetheart," Renee said softly. "So, what time are we meeting tonight?"

"I'll be by your place around seven thirty tonight, so make sure you're good and hungry," he told her. She told him how excited she was about their plans that night and she would look forward to seeing him then. She hung up the phone with a renewed good feeling about the two of them.

Jason realized he still hadn't come up with a final decision on the key party. He figured they could just discuss it over dinner. So far, he was pretty against it, but he wanted to see where Renee stood on things.

His Monday hadn't been too bad, not that he had really been there mentally anyway. His mind was focused on the evening he and Renee would be spending together. All he had to do was finish up some research he was doing on a case he had been working on for months. It was a case involving sexual abuse between a father and his kids and the mother was filing for divorce. These were especially hard cases for him. He decided to let it wait until tomorrow and headed out of the office to get ready for his date.

It was already five o'clock and he still had to go pick up some flowers and wine. On the way to the store he asked himself what his reservations were as far as the party was concerned. He knew he didn't want Renee to feel inhibited or hindered by his concerns in any way. He tried to think of it as being harmless. Just something to spice up the relationship even. He was hoping she would be a little apprehensive so that he didn't seem like the skeptical one. Well, they would discuss it later. At least he knew where he stood on things. He would say no. But if Renee was for it, then he was too.

Renee left her office at 4:00 p.m. She worked as an executive for a small advertising company. She said good-bye to Sandra and Lisa, who worked with her, and headed to the parking garage. She was really excited about the night; she already had her outfit picked out and her lingerie was "banging." She planned to wear a dress she had gotten from Nordstrom's. It was gold with gold beads that hung from the hem at the bottom and came well past her knees. She knew Jason preferred long skirts or dresses to minis. She had bought a pair of Manolo Blahnik shoes from Nieman Marcus that put her out $675, but this was a special night. Her manicure and pedicure were still holding up from earlier in the week, so all she needed was to take a shower and do her hair. She couldn't wait to see what Jason had been thinking in terms of the key party. In all honesty, she really didn't think he would go for it. He was *so* protective of her. He always had been. She just couldn't see him agreeing to her sleeping with another man. She already knew he would beat around the bush and eventually say he didn't think it was in their best interest. Renee, on the other hand, thought it was a cool idea. They were all such good friends and she knew it wasn't about falling in love. She had always wanted to let loose and just let herself go without calculating what would happen every single step of the way. She was the more reserved one between herself and Kay. She already knew Kay would be ready and willing, and for once in her life, she wanted to be "down" too. She was going to see what Jason thought first so she wouldn't completely embarrass herself. Oh well, no use dwelling on it until they were together to discuss it. She ran up the stairs of her complex and started getting ready for the evening.

"So, Nikki, have you gotten any confirmations on the party yet?" Chris shouted from the living room. Nikki was busy working on an assignment for work.

"I'm sorry, hon, what did you say?"

"I was asking about the party, has anyone called about it yet?"

"Oh, not yet. My guess is that they're going to give it some serious thought over the weekend and then let me know by the middle of next week." Nikki was thinking that Kay and Kevin would be down for sure. Lynda would probably convince Rick that it would be harmless and might add some spice to their sex life. Chris had come to terms with it after lots of conversation, but she just wasn't sure about Jason and Renee. She knew that Renee would consider it at least, but figured Jason would probably be hesitant and they'd end up backing out. As for Kevin and Kay, she knew they would be in.

Kay was always interested in something scandalous and Kevin was just trying to keep up with her.

The phone rang for a second time. "Hello," Nikki said.

"Hey, girl!" It was Lynda. "What are you guys up to tonight?" she said, sounding like she was already juiced up.

"Nothing, I'm doing some paperwork I brought home and Chris is watching golf. It's safe to say that neither of us is busy. Why, what are you guys up to?"

"Nothing, just wondering if you wanted to meet up at that new sushi spot on Pharr Road. I know it's not your favorite, but you can eat the fried stuff you had last time. We kind of wanted to talk about this key party and were wondering if you could meet us."

Nikki smiled. At least people were thinking about it. "Cool, girly, what time?"

"How does seven thirty sound?"

Nikki told Lynda they would be there. Chris must have heard the conversation, because he had gotten up and was in the shower before Nikki hung up the phone. Nikki threw her papers on the floor and got undressed. She surprised Chris, jumping in the shower with him to catch a quickie before dinner.

"I know for sure that bijou is a word," Kay said. She and Kevin were spending a quiet evening at home playing Scrabble and watching movies. They rented *The Best Man*, which included her two favorite things: drama and Morris Chestnut!

"Damn, that brother is fine! What more could you say?" Kay laughed, staring at the cover of the *Best Man* video. Her attraction for him was definitely influenced by Kevin. Or was it the other way around? Kay thought to herself. Kevin resembled him in lots of ways. The milk chocolate complexion, his firm, solid build, and last but not least, those beautiful teeth.

"Where are you going?" Kay said.

Kevin was on his feet. "I'm going to get the dictionary. I'm sick of you cheating, girl!"

"Cheating? Cheating? Whatever, Kevin," Kay said, rolling her eyes. "Just because I'm beating you doesn't mean I'm cheating. It's spelled B.I.J.O.U," she told him in a know-it-all voice.

"I know how to spell it, Kay," he told her with attitude in his tone.

"Okay, okay, okay," she said, holding her hands up and backing away slowly. He looked so serious holding that stupid dictionary.

She decided to lighten things up. She ran and jumped on his back. She had completely caught him off guard. He threw her on the couch and started to tickle her mercilessly. That was Kay's weakness and Kevin knew it. She hated being tickled.

"Stop!" Kay said, barely able to breathe. He finally let her up after bringing her to the point of almost peeing in her pants.

"Dang, Kevin, you play too much," she told him, trying to look mad.

They both must have smelled the chicken at the same time, because they ran toward the oven. They had caught it just in time. Kevin said he'd go ahead and set the table for dinner while Kay heated up the yellow rice, green beans, and mashed potatoes. They both enjoyed just chilling with each other. She knew they were both ready to talk about the party, but didn't know how to bring it up. She decided to just go ahead and put it out there.

"So, Kevin, what are your thoughts on this key-party thing?"

"Well, baby, you know me. I love sex. And the more sex, the better. As long as I don't pick Lynda I'm cool."

"Oh, shut up, Kevin," Kay said, throwing a napkin at him.

"She's mean as hell to me," Kevin said, looking like a wounded puppy dog.

"No, she's not, you guys just never really hit it off. She really seems to like you when we get together for girl talk, and I know she likes that tight ass of yours."

Kevin almost choked on his rice. Kay scooted his water closer to him.

"You're crazy, girl," Kevin said, smiling at her.

"Seriously, though, it sounds like fun to me as long as people don't try to get all serious and shit. You know how *that* goes." She knew he was taking a miniature jab at her for cussing his ass out about the spin-the-bottle incident. She refused to let him bait her on that one.

"Yeah, I know what you mean!"

Kevin asked her what she thought about the idea. He just knew her answer would be all dramatic and shit.

"Well," Kay said, trying to tone her shit down since she knew Kevin was expecting her to be a drama queen. "I think it's cool. We can do it if you want."

"So, is it a go then?" Kevin asked to be absolutely sure. "You're willing to share all this chocolate with one of your girls?" he said, rubbing his chest.

He was *so* silly, she thought to herself, smiling.

"Cool, I have one question for you, though. What if it's Renee?" he asked as innocently as he possibly could.

Kay looked completely stunned and he realized that until that very moment, the thought had never even crossed her mind.

"What do you mean?" Kay asked. "You wouldn't do that, would you?"

Kevin felt like he was being cornered. He had been asked trick questions like these in past relationships, but this was two times as tricky and he always ended up putting his hands *and* his feet in his mouth.

"Look, Kay, we cannot agree to this thing and try to have boundaries. There are no boundaries in this. Either we do it or we don't," he said, growing frustrated. "I mean, how long are you going to hold that bullshit against me? Like I told you then, yeah, Renee is a beautiful woman who happens to look just like you, but I'm with you. Yeah, my dick got hard in a closet with our bodies touching, but I'm a fucking man. All man! Get over that shit. I'm with you because I want to be with you. If you don't get that shit by now you never will. I refuse to keep explaining myself," he said. "So last question, Kay, are we in or are we out? If you say we're in, you need to make sure you've considered the possibility of me picking Renee's key. If you need to think about it, then do it and let me know what we're going to do tomorrow."

"Fine," she said, getting up from the table and going to her room.

Kevin was left sitting there in the midst of the shambles wondering what the hell had just happened. He thought he could hear her crying, and normally that shit would bring him to his knees. He couldn't continue to baby Kay, though; she would start using that against him eventually. He replayed the argument over and over in his head.

He never lied to Kay. He loved her very much and wanted to be with her. What he had *never* told her was that at the club where he met her almost a year ago, he had actually wanted Renee first.

She had been sitting alone sipping on a glass of wine and had absolutely taken his breath away. He watched her for about five minutes in silence just observing her every move. Finally, his feet started walking toward her table across the room. "You wanna dance?" he said to her, somehow getting the courage to open his mouth and speak. Renee looked up from her drink and saw Kevin standing there. He could tell she had immediately fallen in love with his smile. He had always been told that his smile was his best feature.

"Oh, no, thanks, I don't dance," she said. He extended his hand and introduced himself. "I'm Kevin."

She smiled hesitantly at first and then stuck her hand out toward him. "I'm Renee."

He bought her a drink and they had talked and laughed for about thirty minutes when he realized he had to go to the bathroom really bad. He must have had like five beers since he had gotten there; his bladder couldn't be failing him at a worst time. They shared a lot of the same interests, basketball and their love for cheese-burgers. Her hair was long and dark and her skin was luminous. He felt like he could stand there and look at her all day. The music had gotten louder suddenly.

"Kevin," she said as she pointed toward the dance floor, at someone coming out of the crowd.

"Yeah?" He had heard her say something about wanting to introduce him to someone, but he had already turned around to go find the restroom. "Hold that thought," he said, telling her he'd be right back. He was hurrying up for fear that he would come out and she would be gone. When he returned, the crowd in front of the bar had cleared out, and he realized that she was gone. Her empty wineglass was all that was left. He felt this sick feeling in the pit of his stomach. How could he have let her go so easily! "Damn!"

He was completely devastated; she had been his dream girl. It had been a while since he'd had such a strong positive vibe about a woman, especially one he had met in a club. He was replaying the conversation in his head when he decided to take one last chance and look around for her. He was in a slight daze when he felt the tap on his shoulder. He spun around and almost fell right over. There *was* a God! She was standing right in front of him. It was like he was looking at a ghost. He couldn't even speak. She had this glow about her as if she had been dancing pretty hard out there. He could have sworn she had turned him down for an invitation to dance. He wouldn't hold that against her, though.

"Hello," she said.

"I thought I'd lost you . . . um . . . I mean, I thought you left," Kevin stuttered.

"I'm sorry, have we met?" the woman asked.

"Stop playing, Renee."

Then it hit her.

"I'm a twin and my sister is here somewhere. You must have been talking to her earlier." She put her hand out to shake his. "My name is Kay. Kay Campbell."

He was still in shock over all this, feeling like a fool. "K-K-Kevin, Kevin Chambers." He was totally confused and it must have shown, because she asked him if there was something wrong.

"You must have met my sister earlier or something. That's usually what happens," she said, looking down. Kevin was holding his forehead as if he had a headache.

"She just left real quick to go grab her fiancé so we

can go get something to eat. I figured I'd say hello since you looked so sad . . . Did you lose your wallet or something?"

"No," he said, but ironically he did feel as if he had lost something more valuable than cash and credit cards. He finally looked up to see that she was just as beautiful as Renee. Gorgeous even! Her hair was pinned up and there were curls all over the place doing their own thing. Renee's hair had been pulled back in a ponytail, which really showed off her cheeks and eyes. This chick appeared to be the prettier one of the two, no doubt.

Kevin realized he was looking real crazy and had to think of something cool to say to save face.

"So where is *your* fiancé?" Kevin said, leaning into Kay a bit.

She could tell he was amused with himself.

"I don't have one, *Kevin*," she said jokingly.

"You don't have one, huh?" he said, looking away.

"That's what I said." Kay snapped her fingers, looking him directly in the eye.

Hmmmmm, he thought. She had a little bite to her . . . he didn't mind, though. She was so adorable it definitely balanced the *attitude* out. He would make an exception this time.

Kevin saw Renee and her fiancé coming their way. "I guess it's time for you to go," he said, grabbing Kay's hand, then letting it go. He knew she hadn't expected him to touch her and that his gesture had thrown her off a bit.

"Renee is my sister, not my mother. I would stay if I had a reason to," she said, looking at him coyly.

"Whatever," Kevin said, laughing that one off.

"Kevin, this is my sister, Renee, and her fiancé, Jason, but I understand you've already met."

"Very nice to meet you both. Good seeing you again," he said, looking at Renee mischievously. His and Renee's eyes locked and they made a silent agreement to disregard the events that had transpired earlier in the evening.

"Kevin? Kevin?" He could hear Kay now. "Would you care to join us for some gourmet after-clubbing cuisine? We're going to IHOP to grab a bite."

"Yeah, let's roll," he answered quickly.

Only he and Renee knew what had happened that night . . . that they had made a small connection. Before he even knew that she had a fiancé, or a twin for that matter. Damn, it was too much to think about at times. He heard Kay crying in the other room and got up from his seat at the table. He couldn't stand to see her upset!

Lynda and Rick saw Nikki and Chris pulling up from their window seat at the Sushi Bar. They had been having a great evening together. Rick was being especially attentive to Lynda these days since her business was slow. She'd been a personal trainer for years and still hadn't gotten used to the fact that her business would always come to a standstill during the months of November and December. Nobody wanted to think about getting in shape when they were looking forward to stuffing their faces with turkey and dressing. He came home from work with the cutest red teddy bear holding balloons that said *Still in Love*.

She really did love Rick. It seemed like they had been together for an eternity. There had always been something missing, though, and deep down, she knew what it was. For one thing, there were lots of improvements needed in the bedroom. They hardly ever made love these days. She was always tired or not in the mood. She knew it was starting to get to him, but she just wasn't motivated. They had just started going to marriage counseling to try and sort some things out.

"Hey, girl." Lynda got up to give Nikki a big hug. She hadn't seen her since the previous weekend and had only talked to her once during the week. Chris gave her a hug and kiss on the cheek.

"Were my directions pretty good"? Lynda asked.

"Ah . . . yeah . . . right," Chris said. "Rick must have given you those directions to give to us," he joked.

"Whatever, Chris," Lynda said, pretending to stab his hand with her fork. She picked up her menu.

"Okay," she said, "who is going to be the brave soul tonight and eat some raw stuff with me?"

"Don't even look at me," Nikki said, "you know all I eat are those fried salmon ones and the California rolls." Rick raised his arm to get the waiter's attention so they could go ahead and order.

"So you guys wanted to discuss the key party? What about it?" Nikki asked.

"Well, what if things are never the same again?" Lynda said with a concerned look on her face. "I mean, what if the group is destroyed after this goes down? It's just not worth it. Do you know anyone who's done this before?"

"I do," Rick said. "This guy at my job told me that he and his wife did it years ago with their tight-knit group of friends. Turns out they were swingers, so I don't know if they count." The guy had told Rick that it made group gatherings a lot more interesting.

"And that's exactly what I see it doing for us," Nikki said. "Even if Rick happened to pull my name, I love Chris and all it would be is one night and then it's over.

The way I see it is like this, Lynda. I asked myself if I could live with the worst-case scenario, which for me is Chris pulling your name since we're best friends." The men were quiet. "I wondered if I could live with it, knowing that my husband and my best friend shared a special night together. A secret night that I'll never know anything about."

"And what did you come up with?" Lynda asked.

"Well, I can only speak for myself. I could live with it all."

"That's the same thing I told her," Rick mumbled.

"Well, isn't this essentially swinging, though?" Lynda asked.

"I don't think so. I mean, swingers see casual sex as a lifestyle, and I think they have sex with strangers as well as friends," Nikki said. "This is different. We all know each other pretty well and we are all such good friends and it's just one night!"

"Yeah, you're right. Well, I'm in. I wanna go for it. It sounds fun. What do you guys think about the whole thing?" Lynda said, waiting for Chris and Rick to answer.

"Um, I . . . I mean . . . it's cool, you know. It's pretty freaky, you know, but that's what we get for dealing with you ladies, right?" Rick said, smiling.

"Yup!" Lynda said, giving Nikki a high five. "That's what you get!"

Their food arrived just in time. Lynda felt a lot better about the whole thing. She and Rick gave Nikki their verbal confirmation right then and there.

The next morning, Nikki was running late for work at the news station. She had studied public relations and advertising through college but decided after an internship with a PR firm that it just wasn't for her. The only good thing that came out of it was meeting Chris. She changed majors and would eventually finish at Clark University, graduating with honors from their journalism program. She got on with one of the biggest news stations in Atlanta by a stroke of good luck. One of the big dogs from their human resources department had remembered Nikki from way back when she was paying her dues at the PR firm. When she saw Nikki's name come across her desk, she called her for an interview for an apprentice position to one of the more seasoned newscasters. Nikki had accepted with no hesitation. She knew it would be grunt work, but that's how these types of jobs worked, you had to pay your dues and just wait for your opportunity to come. She had actually gotten the opportunity to cover a couple of stories in the year since she had been there. Nothing too exciting, one was a story about asbestos in schools and the safety concerns involved, the other had been about a pyramid scandal that had made its way back onto the scene, the one where people give their hard-earned money and hope to end up at the top of the pyramid and get paid.

When she got to work she immediately started working on some research for Sherry Heart, a reporter who was pretty much her boss. Sherry had asked her to do some research on the rat problem in Atlanta. She was busting her ass to find any info she could on the problem for Sherry's story. She was almost finished when she realized she was supposed to be having lunch with Kay and Renee at the mall, then leave them to do their fall clothes shopping together. She dug all around the dark pit she called a purse and found her cell phone.

She dialed Renee at work and was elated to hear her answer.

"Hello?"

"Is that how you answer your company's phone?" Nikki said jokingly.

"Whatever, girl, I can see it's your crazy ass on the caller ID. What's up? You canceling on us?"

"No, not at all, I just may be running ten minutes late or so and wanted to give you a heads-up."

"Okay, no problem, we'll see you around one thirty then."

"Cool, bye!"

Kay had one house to show that morning to a gentleman named Brian Carter. She was meeting him at nine-thirty, so she needed to get up. She absolutely loved the flexibility of the real estate business. She was supposed to hook up with Kevin for cocktails later that night so they could smooth things over a bit. It was a make-up dinner. At the moment, she was still in bed watching *Jenny Jones* when the phone rang.

"Hey, sis," Kay said, knowing it was Renee on the other end. Kay was hoping Renee wasn't calling to back out of lunch now that she was looking forward to it. Renee just wanted to confirm that they were meeting at Lenox Mall at one thirty. Kay told her she would see her then. Since their talk the other night, they had gotten a little closer and Kay realized how lost she would be without Renee. There was nothing she wouldn't do for her. That's why she was cringing at the sight of these sisters fighting like men in front of millions of people on *Jenny Jones*. Their argument was classic. One of the sisters had slept with her sister's man and decided to come on national TV and be honest about it. *Whatever,* Kay thought. That was the craziest shit she'd ever seen. These talk shows had really gotten out of hand, but for some reason she watched them whenever she could. She waited for the credits to roll before she pulled herself out of bed to go take a shower.

She was going over in her head what she needed to buy at the mall while she took her shower. She had spotted this really nice Movado watch that Kevin had his eye on. It cost like $895 but she knew he really wanted it. Luckily, she'd had an exceptional month, closing on four houses. The extra money that she would see on this paycheck would allow her to splurge just a bit. Besides, she hadn't bought him anything in a while. Kay wanted to hurry up and get out of the house to take care of a couple of things before lunch.

Renee's day had been uneventful; things had been slow since the summer actually. She didn't mind, though, as it gave her time to get caught up on old projects in an attempt to clean house before the new year. By the time she looked up, it was already noon. She would be leaving in an hour to meet Kay and Nikki. Her dinner with Jason had been fabulous the night before.

He had picked her up at seven thirty so they would arrive right on time for their eight o'clock reservations at Park Place. The food was delicious and the conversation very light and enjoyable. Jason brought her up to speed on a case he was working on. A woman was trying to get full custody of her two children, accusing the father of the children of sexual abuse. Renee could see that the case was starting to affect Jason. To lighten the mood, they had even discussed the key party. At first Jason wasn't too happy about the idea of her having sex with another man, but when she told him that she wanted to live a little and do something unexpected of her, he to her surprise changed his mind. She saw it as a chance to live on the edge for once and was excited about it. Jason had reminded Renee to call Nikki to let her know they were all for the key party.

Kay and Nikki got to the mall at the same time. They always ate at the same spot . . . California Pizza Kitchen. They sat down and ordered their drinks, then started catching up until they saw Renee headed their way.

"Hey, sis," Kay said, excited to see her twin.

"Hey, Kay, Hey, Nikki," Renee said. "Did you guys order already?"

"Not yet, we were waiting for you."

"Cool, let's order. I'm starving. So, what's been up, Kay?" Nikki asked. "Where are you coming from?"

"Oh yeah, I had a house to show this morning. This guy was a real cutie too. His name was Brian Carter, single, no kids, looking at a six-bedroom house. If I was single he would be in big trouble. It seemed kind of weird to me that a bachelor would need that much space, but judging by the Jaguar he was in I assumed he has money to burn."

"Cool," Nikki said.

"So do you think he'll buy?" Renee asked Kay.

"I don't know. I usually get a pretty good vibe when I feel like a person is really interested. It almost seemed like he was just going through the motions. We'll see, though. You know me and my follow-up skills," Kay said. "If I can't close him, no one can. That's if he's serious about buying. But enough about me, what have you two been up to?"

"Well, I've just been waiting for my phone to ring," Nikki said, throwing hints about the key party.

"Yeah, you should be getting a call from me soon," Renee said confidently. Kay looked surprised.

"You're going to do it?" Kay asked.

"Yeah, I know," Renee said, "you guys had already counted me and Jason out. Fooled all of you, ha! Maybe I'll learn a couple of tricks that I can use on my honeymoon next year," she said, smiling.

"Damn, Renee, you got me this time," Kay said. "I just knew you were going to give us some lame story about it not being the 'right' thing to do, et cetera, et cetera."

"I know, Kay," Renee said, "I like to keep you all guessing, that's all."

"Yeay," Nikki said. "I'm so glad you guys are in. So Jason was all right with it too?"

"Well, he hesitated for a second, but when he saw that I was down he was down."

"He's got you *so* spoiled," Nikki said proudly.

"I know. He just wants to make me happy. That's all. Have you heard from Lynda yet?" Renee asked Nikki.

"Yup, me and Chris had dinner with her and Rick the other night and they're in."

If nothing else, Kay's sheer surprise had been worth Renee's decision to go forward with this whole thing. She was tired of being so predictable, Renee thought. If they only knew what Kay's hesitation had been they would be so disappointed that she still held a grudge for so long. It went deeper than that, though. Even though Kay was always considered the prettier one of the two, Renee's personality had always paid off for her in the long run. Kay was also the older by four minutes and fourteen seconds. Renee had always been the more practical of the two of them. She had a good head on her shoulders and always made good, sound decisions.

"So you guys realize that this thing is really going to happen, right?" Nikki asked excitedly.

"I know," Renee said, "and I'm actually starting to get used to the idea of it all."

Four

Mr. Campbell's Visit

The night Kay and Renee found out their mother had been killed was their worst memory ever. They'd had a basketball game that night and their mom wasn't feeling well. She suffered from really bad migraine headaches. It was their most critical game of the entire season, the one that would secure their spot in the championship game. All they had left were the play-offs and then the championship game. Their mom, Rachel, had never missed a game. They had tried real hard to convince her to go, saying that her headache would wear off after she got out in the fresh air. Not even their dad could get her to change her mind. The girls had been upset, especially Kay. On their way out the door, Kay barely hugged her mother and gave her one of those weak kisses on the cheek. Even as they were walking to the car Rachel was apologizing for not being able to go.

"Karl," Rachel yelled after them, "be careful, it's rain-

ing out there. Take care of my girls!" She always said
that if they were going somewhere without her.

"I will, Rachel, I always do," their dad said, blowing a
kiss Rachel's way.

On the way home from the game, they had passed
the accident without even knowing it. They were too
busy celebrating the victory in the car. They couldn't
wait to show their mom the trophy. When they got into
the house the phone was ringing.

"Hello?" their dad said. "Yes, this is Karl Campbell.
Rachel? That's my wife, yes. *What?*" They watched their
father become completely undone right before their
eyes. "There has to be a mistake," he said, sounding desperate. "Well, no . . . no . . . she's not here. Maybe she just
went to the store . . . Are you sure? . . . Are you sure it
says Rachel Campbell?" he asked, hoping for a miracle.
"There's a bag of what? A prescription lying next to
her? Damn it." She had asked him to pick that up for
her on his way home and he forgot. She had run out of
the house to pick up her migraine medicine. Now she
would never see another day.

Renee had been the one to calm Kay and her dad
down after he hung up the phone. He had to collect
himself; he had to go identify the body. He had the girls
go next door to a neighbor's house while he made the
lonely drive. Renee comforted Kay all night long, holding her in her arms like a newborn, rocking her back
and forth until the crying and shaking subsided. Renee
sobbed all night too, but she had to be strong for Kay
and her dad. That's what her mom would have wanted.
She knew that.

The girls were never the same. Their personalities
seemed to travel to two different extremes after their
mother's death. Kay became rather wild and Renee be-

came an introvert. Before that, they had been inseparable. To this day their dad had not really recovered. He never remarried and the thought of what had happened could still bring tears to his eyes. It was a heartbreaking sight. It truly was.

"Kay, what's wrong?" Renee said, looking at her sister.

"Huh?" Kay said, realizing she had taken a short trip down memory lane in the middle of their lunch. "I'll be right back. I just need to run to the restroom."

"What's with her?" Nikki said with a concerned look on her face.

"Um, I don't know, probably just PMS," Renee said. She knew Kay must have been thinking about their mom. It happened every now and then at the most unexpected times.

Kay came back rejuvenated and ready to shop. They didn't mention what had just happened, they just moved on with their conversation.

Jason was exhausted but knew he had one more stop to make before he could go home. He still had to pick up Renee's surprise. He was on his way to the airport to pick up her dad. She hadn't seen him in a couple of years and she missed him tremendously. The last time she called was to tell him that she and Jason were engaged to be married. Jason had only heard about him, he'd never met him. They had stopped visiting when he told them it made things even more difficult for him. They were the spitting image of their mom. Kay knew he was coming, but they had kept it a secret from

Renee. He would only stay the weekend, but it would be the gift that kept on giving, Jason was sure of it. He knew Karl's flight was due in at 8:15 p.m. That gave him an hour to go home and change before heading toward Kay's place to scoop her up and then head to the airport. Renee wasn't expecting Jason until much later that night. He told her he had a lot to do for the case he was working on and that he would be by sometime after nine o'clock.

When they arrived at baggage claim, Kay pointed her dad out almost immediately. He hadn't waited at the gate like Jason told him to. He made the trek to the baggage area by himself. His smile widened from ear to ear when Kay rolled down the window and yelled, "Daddy!"

She jumped out and hugged his neck so tightly he dropped his bags.

"Slow down, baby girl," he said. "I'm back on the block and I'm not going anywhere, darling." He kissed her forehead. She was as beautiful as he had remembered. But there was something missing. He needed to see the last piece of this puzzle . . . Renee.

Jason walked around the car and put his hand out for Karl to shake. He shook it firmly and then gave him a big bear hug.

"So, you're the one who's trying to take my daughter away from me, huh?" Karl said jokingly.

Jason knew he was only kidding, but coming from such a tall guy with a firm build like Mr. Campbell's, he still answered as respectfully as possible.

"Sir, I'm going to give your daughter the world if it's

the last thing I do. I mean whatever is left of the world since I'm sure you've given her the world all these years." Jason was mumbling now. Kay jabbed him in the side with her elbow.

"Let's get out of here," Karl said. "I hate airports!"

Renee was hoping Jason would be there soon. She hadn't planned anything too special. She put on one of his favorite pieces of lingerie, a two-piece red sheer getup that drove him wild. She poured some wine and had the mood set with a little Luther playing. She was in the mood for some stress-relieving romance that night. She had gotten up a couple of times thinking she heard his car pull up in front of her window. She was on the first floor of the complex. Her dad would kill her if he knew she lived on that level. He spent most of his life worrying about his girls.

The loud knock at the door scared the shit out of her. She had been in the bathroom making sure everything was in place. She looked out of the peephole and saw Jason standing there cheesing. She flung the door open, standing their looking like she was ready for some good lovin'. To her chagrin she saw her sister standing before her with her eyes and mouth wide open. Jason only had remnants of the cheesy smile she had seen through the peephole, and her dad had his hand over his mouth.

"*Ahhhhhhhhhhhhhh!*" Renee screamed, running to the back of her apartment to her bedroom. Her dad, Jason, and Kay came in and closed the door behind them. Jason could have sworn that Karl had given him the evil eye. He obviously didn't want to have a visual of how his daughter got sexy for her man. Renee came out about five minutes later looking as if she had been caught with her hand in the cookie jar. Her dad got up and hugged her.

"Don't worry about all that, dear. That's what I get for trying to surprise you, now, isn't it?" he said, smiling. Renee was still apologizing profusely.

"All right already," Kay said. "I mean, it's okay . . . don't feel bad, Renee. Dad came all the way here to see us."

Kay made Renee sick sometimes. She just had a knack for saying the wrong things at the wrong time. The only thing that usually saved her was the fact that Renee knew she meant well.

"Are you surprised?" Jason said, pointing at Karl.

"Ahhh, yeah . . . I'm very happy, Jason, and very surprised."

"That's all I needed to hear," Jason told Renee, giving her a kiss.

"Well, I'm going to leave you three to do some catching up. I'll be by to pick you up tomorrow around eleven a.m., Mr. Campbell. We'll do some sightseeing and have lunch."

"Cool, Jay. Can I call you Jay?"

"Yeah, that'll work. I'll see you in the morning."

He kissed Kay and Renee on the cheek and headed out the door. Renee was still in shock. She couldn't believe her dad was there. She didn't realize how much happiness she had been missing out on over the years. Kay was sitting on his lap going through some pictures of her and Kay on a ski trip in Aspen the previous year.

"Dad," Renee yelled from the kitchen, "what do you want to drink?"

"Do you have any beer, sweetie?"

Renee walked into the living room, handing her dad a beer and Kay a wine cooler. She had gotten a cooler for herself as well.

"I know you two are hungry," Renee said. "I'll order pizza. Kay, you're staying, right?" Renee hoped she would stay. Even though they weren't as close as most twins, they cared a great deal for one another.

"Yeah, girl, I'm staying!"

They both laughed. The rest of the night was spent catching up with everyone's lives. It had turned into a *Chicken Soup for the Soul* kind of night and it felt damn good! Kay and Renee had gone to bed around three thirty after their dad got his good-night kisses. It had been so long, he thought . . . too long. It would never be this way again as long as he had life in him. These were his girls . . . his and Rachel's girls. He had to make sure they were okay.

Renee awoke the next morning to the sound of her dad in the kitchen making coffee. It was the best she had felt in a long time, the best surprise ever! Kay's big head was still sleep. Renee called into work sick so she could spend time with her dad.

"Morning, Daddy," Renee said, leaning down to kiss him on the cheek. She loved him so much.

"Hey, darling. I love your little place. It's nice and cozy. You have it decorated real nice too. You always did have real good taste. Remember that time you helped your mother go pick out drapes for . . ." His thoughts wandered and he immediately stopped talking.

"Dad, I want you to do me a favor. If you feel like talking about Mom while you're here, I want you to talk about her. I think we *should* talk about Mom. It's time! She's not some deep, dark secret. She was our mother and your wife. It's okay to talk about her, Dad, it's okay."

He put his hands over his eyes so Renee couldn't see him tearing up.

"It's okay, Dad, we all miss her dearly."

He got it together pretty quickly. "I know, baby, it's just that you guys remind me of her so much. I loved that woman. Loved her to death."

"I know, Dad, but this is going to be good therapy for you. We should celebrate Mom's life while you're here. That should be our goal, okay? Promise me you won't hold back, Dad . . . promise?"

"I promise!"

"Good, now you *need* to get ready for Jason to come pick you up this morning. You guys are hanging all day. Then Kay's boyfriend, Kevin, is meeting up with you guys somewhere later."

"Yes, ma'am, I'll go take a quick shower and then I'll get some breakfast cooked."

Renee laughed, realizing her dad still thought she was fifteen years old. Their mother, Rachel, had never been much of a cook, but she had taken care of them and their dad in other ways.

"Dad, how about if I make breakfast while you're getting ready? Trust me, I can do it!"

"Okay," he said, smiling at Renee. "Okay, baby girl."

No one was answering at Kevin's place, so Jason tried his cell phone. That was odd. It was already nine-fifteen and Kevin had taken the day off as far as Jason knew. Meanwhile Kevin was rolling over in bed about ready to hit the snooze button again, when he realized the phone had been ringing. He knew it was Jason but just couldn't get his eyes open. He was supposed to meet up with him and Kay's dad at a Chicken and Waffle spot off of Peachtree Street around noon. He needed to get up so he could run by his job and grab some paperwork to bring home.

Kevin was the assistant football coach over at Georgia Tech. He knew all about having the NFL dream, living it, and then having it snatched away right from under him. He had actually played in the league for two and a half years. Not quite enough time for him to receive his pension. The league had been good to him for the most part, but no one told him it could be over just like that. He had never been given an explanation as to why he had been cut. He was so devastated when he came home and finally woke up from the dream that he spent most of his time drinking the pain away.

He contacted his old coach at Tech to see if they could use any help on their coaching staff. They told him he would always have a home at Tech. The very next week they put him on the payroll as their assistant head coach. He felt so blessed and really prayed for God to use him in the right way in his position. He wanted to do something different with these boys. He was their coach, but more importantly, he was their friend and they admired and respected him. He would never lie to them like he had been lied to—thinking it would all be gravy at the end of his college career. He spent many nights dozing off in a dorm room trying to help his players cram for final exams in order to pass a class. And that's what he was about. He wanted them to understand how important their education would be when all the glory of football was gone.

He decided to swing by his job after lunch. He could almost smell the chicken and waffles floating through his head. He was ready to eat! He threw on some of his "I'm just here, I'm not trying to hurt anybody" gear and headed toward the restaurant downtown. On the way, he realized that he was actually about to meet Kay's dad for the first time. There wasn't even enough time to be nervous. Kay had never said more than a couple of things about her dad, or any of her family for that matter. Mostly he knew that his name was Karl and that he still lived in South Carolina, in Kay and Renee's hometown. He would just smile his way through this one, making good eye contact. Karl would definitely like him; Kevin had no doubt. He had always been good with the parents of his girlfriends.

Five

Girls' and Guys' Night Out

Chris had been in meetings all day, but nothing could distract him from the fact that it was "spades" night. They usually got together at Kevin's house to play a couple of hands of spades, drink lots of beer, eat pizza, and talk a lot of shit. Mostly talk shit! He checked his watch and saw that it was only four-thirty. He normally stayed in the office until six-thirty or seven, but not tonight. He would go over a presentation he had prepared for the following day to put final touches on it, and then he was out of there. He planned on going straight to Kevin's from work, so he figured he would leave around six so he could stop by the liquor store and pick up some Hennessy and Icehouse. He called Kevin and left a message to let him know he would be there. Just as he hung up, his phone started ringing.

"What's up, Rick? Am I going? Man, I'll be there, no doubt. I'm trying to finish up some stuff now, and then I'm headed over there. Are *you* going? You know how Lynda doesn't like you to be out of the house by yourself," Chris said, laughing. "I'm just playing, man. All right, well, I'll see you at seven with liquor and beer in my hand. Peace!"

Lynda was on the phone with her mother-in-law when Rick came down the stairs. "It's your mom," she said, gesturing for him to come take the phone from her. Rick waved both of his hands, and whispered back at Lynda that he was leaving. Lynda rolled her eyes at him, realizing she would be stuck on the damn phone for at least another fifteen minutes. Rick's mother had always been long-winded. He yelled from the door that he loved her and was gone. She knew what his plans were for the night: spades with the fellas. It was the guys' monthly ritual, so to speak. They always tried to have at least one card night a month unless they were just too terribly busy. These were nights when Lynda rented two or three movies and kicked back, taking full advantage of being alone. It was already six-thirty and she was still on the phone longing for her bathtub full of steaming hot water. She had placed scented candles all around her garden tub; cucumber melon was her absolute favorite. She could finally see light at the end of the tunnel for her phone call. She hung the phone up in sheer delight and ran up the stairs to get to that hot bath. She just wanted to free her mind and not think at all. She took off everything and looked at the pile of clothes that lay there on the floor containing all of the stress and headache in her life. She put her right foot in first and it burned so good. She laid her head back and closed her eyes. She completely submerged her shoulders and then let her entire body sink down in the water.

Her thoughts wandered from Rick to her realization that the key party was only a week away. Rick had wanted to talk about things that were discussed in therapy when they got home, and by then Lynda was exhausted. She just didn't feel like talking about their troubles after all that. She had to admit, though, it really had helped things along. The energy between them wasn't so stiff and tense all the time. Things had relaxed between them quite a bit. She could tell they were both letting their guard down after many years of holding back. She was happy about it too. She missed the old Rick and Lynda, and for a long time she hadn't realized that they were even gone.

She wondered how Nikki was doing. She had talked to her briefly the night before, but Nikki was busy with work as usual. They were such good friends, but Lynda wished they had more time to spend together. Since October was coming to a close, Lynda had started full force with promotions for her personal training semi-nars. She was pushing fliers, handing out coupons, and doing other things that were all a part of her annual routine to help market herself. The business had been lucrative for her, but word of mouth had proven to be her best method of marketing, so she had to make sure people knew what she had to offer.

She and Nikki used to work out together before Nikki had become a "career woman." They used to meet after work at a fitness center near the mall three days a week. It had been great; they were able to spend time together and Lynda was able to give Nikki tips on work-ing out. Not that Nikki needed much work. She was about a size 8, Lynda figured. She ate pretty healthy and was able to maintain that figure effortlessly.

As Lynda began to relax, she got ready to begin one

of her other rituals during her Calgon moments. She pushed her hand under the water toward her "spot." She was always surprised at how good she could always make herself feel. She never rushed things in the least, just took her time and enjoyed every single feeling that came with giving herself pleasure. She usually didn't think about anything in particular when she was in the process of bringing herself to ecstasy, but this time she saw Nikki's face. Not only did she see her face, but she also saw her breasts, and her thighs, and it made her want to come stronger and harder. She imagined how Nikki smelled and felt. "Mmmmmm." She was almost there now, but she didn't want the visions of Nikki to be gone . . . she couldn't contain herself any longer . . . she was going to scream if she didn't just let it go . . . "Ah . . . ah . . . ah . . . ahhh-hhhhhhhhhhhhhhhhhhh . . . oh yes . . . yes . . . it feels so good."

In her moment of heaven, she realized that the phone had rung for the third time and she rushed to pick it up. She took her hand out of the water and grabbed the phone on the wall next to the tub. She tried to regain her composure.

"He . . . hello?"

"Hey, Lynda" It was Nikki! "Are you busy?"

"Hey, girl," Lynda said calmly as if she hadn't violated poor Nikki in her fantasy just seconds ago. "No, just getting out of the tub and about to get dressed."

"Yeah, I'm just going to chill tonight, too."

"You sound like you've got something on your mind."

"Nah, I just don't feel like being alone tonight, that's all."

"Well, let's go grab some drinks and something to eat, then . . . your choice." She could hear Nikki's smile through the phone.

"Cool, I'll meet you at that Bahama Breeze place by the mall. Their drinks are the bomb and the music is nice."

"Okay, meet you there in an hour. Oh, first two drinks are on me." She chuckled to herself and hung up the phone, which was covered in soap bubbles.

Jason and Kevin were dropping Karl off at Renee's, getting ready to head back to Kevin's place. They didn't have a lot of time to chitchat, so they headed upstairs, both agreeing to get in and out of there as quickly as possible.

"Well, thanks for a real enjoyable day, gentleman," Karl said, shaking their hands firmly. Jason and Kevin both grinned and smiled their way out the door to freedom.

"Phew, let's roll, man," Kevin said as they both ran down Renee's apartment stairs.

Jason decided to ride with Kevin to his place instead of taking two cars. He figured Rick could drop him off on his way back home since they lived on the same side of town.

Lauryn Hill's duet with Bob Marley was ending on Hot 97.5. When that went off, they played a real oldie but goodie. "I love this shit," Kevin said. It was an old Slick Rick song that Kevin hadn't heard in years, "Children's Story." Kevin was in his own world, reciting each verse as if he had written it. Jason was busy laughing at him.

"I've been looking forward to this night all month, man," Jason said.

"I hear that. So what . . . work got you all stressed out?"

"To say the least. I've been working on this case for-ever and now that it's finally over, it looks like the guy I'm prosecuting is going to get off. I think I'll lose my damn mind if he does."

"Damn, man, you obviously put a lot into it, and that's all you could do. It won't be the last case you lose, so you've got to start embracing your losses, as few as they may be. I know the feeling, though, man, I've got some bullshit going on at my job too that I wish I could just run away from. I just try to stay positive, though, and re-mind myself that it has to get better. I refuse to let any-thing get me down tonight. So try to get your mind right for this ass whupping we're about to give to Chris and Rick," Kevin said jokingly. "Just try to let everything else go and enjoy yourself tonight. Once the liquor gets a hold of you, you won't have a choice anyway," he said, smiling and elbowing Jason in the side.

"What time is it, man? I left my watch sitting right on top of my desk at work," Jason said, frowning. "I'm glad I have an office or I know one of the janitors would be having a field day with my shit."

"It's about ten till seven. Rick and Chris should be pulling up any minute now if they're not already here," Kevin said as he turned into his subdivision. His house was the last one on the left all the way at the end of the little cul-de-sac. It was the first thing he bought when he had signed his contract with the Steelers. That had been his proudest accomplishment to date.

Rick was already there, parked and waiting in his car. He waved as they pulled into the driveway.

"What's going on, fellas?" Rick said, giving Jason and Kevin a pound.

"Nothing, man, just ready to chill and run these cards for a couple of hours," Kevin said, smiling deviously. He and Jason were always beating the hell out of Chris and Rick. "Let's get inside," Kevin said. They all agreed and walked into the house. Before they could get their coats off good, the door opened and Chris walked in. He was holding up the liquor and beer he had stopped to get on the way.

"My contribution for the night, fellas," Chris said.

"That's *what* I'm talking about," Kevin said, "a man that comes prepared. What do you guys want on this pizza? Hurry up, the guy has me on hold." They all just yelled out their favorite toppings. Kevin ordered two large pizzas with pepperoni, Italian sausage, and mushrooms.

Kevin hung up with the pizza place and got up to cut on the lights in the den. Next he turned on the stereo system. That was one thing Kevin did not play about; he loved his music.

"So what kind of mood are you guys in tonight?" Kevin asked the guys, pointing his CD remote at the receiver. "Y'all want to hear a little Joe?"

"Hell no, man," Rick yelled from the kitchen, fixing a drink. They all slept on Joe. Kevin tried to tell them that Joe was the next Luther, but they weren't trying to hear it.

"Well, I'll just start us off with a little bit of Master P for now."

"That'll work," all the guys said at the same time.

"Cool, I'll run upstairs and get the cards. You guys get some paper and a pen to keep score."

Nikki was sitting at the bar listening to the Caribbean music, enjoying the scenery at Bahama Breeze. She couldn't wait to see Lynda. She wished that Kay and

Renee could have made it too, but she knew their dad was in town keeping them busy. Nikki was on her second margarita when someone grabbed her from behind. She turned around, startled, and saw Kay, Renee, and Lynda all standing there.

"Hi, girls," Nikki squealed, standing up and giving them all love. "What are you two doing here?"

"I called them after we got off the phone," Lynda said. "You sounded like you needed to see all of us, so I convinced them to come too."

"Yeah, we dropped Dad off at the airport and headed straight here," Kay said.

"I thought he was staying a little longer."

"He was supposed to, but he had a sudden crisis at his job so he had to take the first flight home. He was worn out and almost looked relieved that he was leaving."

Nikki mentioned that she was sad she didn't get a chance to meet Mr. Campbell, but Renee told her he would be coming back to visit in the spring.

"Okay, let's order some drinks," Nikki suggested, swinging around on her bar stool. She raised her hand to get the bartender's attention. "Can we get a round of lemon drops please?"

"Whoa," Renee said, "you must be in a serious drinking mood. We haven't done those in ages."

"That's right! I'm definitely in the mood to get my drink on tonight. You guys with me?"

"Definitely!" Lynda replied.

"Sure thing," Kay said.

"Well, I guess I'm outnumbered. I'm in," Renee said reluctantly. Back in the day they each could have done three lemon drops on top of a half dozen glasses of wine and been good to go.

"Let's get a table," Lynda said, "my feet hurt."

"Well, I want to sit on the patio," Kay said, "it looks like fun out there." They found a table near the bonfire on the patio. It was nice and toasty there.

"I'm loving this music," Lynda said, talking over the music that the band was playing. "Reminds me of my and Rick's honeymoon in Jamaica."

"Yeah, nice choice, Nikki," Kay and Renee said at the same time. Nikki had been there several times with Chris on their date nights and fell in love with the place.

"You all don't know how glad I am to see you," Nikki said.

"I know, this month is going by so fast," Kay said.

"Can you believe the party is next weekend?" Renee asked everyone.

"I hope you ladies aren't gonna back out of it," Nikki told them.

"Uh-uh, no way," Renee said. "I'm seeing this one through to the very end if it's the last thing I do."

"Me too," Kay chimed in.

After they downed their lemon drops, Lynda ordered a round of margaritas on the rocks, no salt.

"I wonder what the guys are doing right about now," Kay said.

"Who knows?" Nikki said. "Probably talking about how big Jennifer Lopez's ass is in her new video."

"No shit," Kay said, "I get so tired of hearing about that one."

"Yeah, Jason isn't even an ass man, so to speak, but let her video come on and it's over for me."

"Do you guys think they're getting hyped up about the party?" Lynda asked.

"Why wouldn't they be?" Kay said. "They get some

new snatch next weekend, no questions asked, are you kidding? Those fools are probably wondering why Nikki waited this long to have the damn party." They all started laughing.

"They're probably not even talking about it," Renee said.

"Right about now, Kevin is probably trying to hype them all up to go to the strip club," Kay said.

"Yeah, trying to hype my baby all up," Renee said, stirring her drink.

"Oh, whatever," Nikki said. "Like Jason needs that much convincing."

"He does, he says he only goes because *your* men always want to be up in there."

"I hope you don't believe that lame shit, Renee," Lynda said, laughing at her. "That's the oldest one in the book."

"Hey, speaking of Jason . . . let me ask you something, Renee. Do you think that he's up for this key party?"

"What do you mean?"

"Well, he's just so . . . let's see, how do I say this?"

"Crazy!" Kay butted in.

"Crazy? What's that supposed to mean?" Renee said, sitting up in her chair.

"No . . . that's not what I was going to say, Renee. Look, Kay, mind your business . . . What I was going to say is that he seems a little high-strung . . . especially when he's drinking. Is he going to be able to hang with this?"

"Oh . . . well . . . yeah, I think so. He'll be fine. It's all in fun. I gotta go to the bathroom," Renee said, excusing herself from the table. She didn't want to talk about Jason with the girls. She knew what Kay and Lynda meant and didn't want to deal with it. She just wanted to have a good time tonight.

"I can't believe you asked her that, Lynda."

"What? Shit, don't pretend you don't know what I'm talking about, Nikki."

"I know, I know, but that's her man. What are we gonna do? Tell him he can't play?"

"Well, I don't know about you, but I would be afraid if he picked my key."

"Ha, ha, you're a mess, Lynda," Kay said. "But I know what you mean. He's so damn cute, but he scares me a little."

"Yeah, that's what I mean. He's a little scary. I mean, would you really want to have sex with him if given the chance?"

"Well, I like Jason," Nikki said on Renee's behalf. "I think he's cute. He's definitely a little nuts when he's drinking, but hell, we're all going to be drinking and a little out of control, so I think that it will be fine. End of story . . . shhhhh . . . here comes Renee."

"Hey, what did I miss?"

"Not a thing, girl. Listen, I have an idea. Why don't we go to the CITY?" Lynda said.

"Go where?" Kay said. "You mean a strip club?"

"Yup, let's go!" Lynda said, getting excited.

"Have you ever been?" Renee asked Lynda.

"Nope, let's do it."

"I've always wondered what goes on in there," Nikki said. "I would love to roll up on Chris's ass like *what, what!*" He would be so shocked."

"I wonder how wild they get," Kay said.

"Let's do it," Lynda said again putting her hand in the middle of the table, holding it in midair. "C'mon, ladies, live a little."

"What the hell?" Nikki said. "I'm in." Kay and Renee were looking at each other.

"Okay, okay," Renee said. "We're in too."

They didn't even notice that the family seated next to them was eavesdropping on their conversation and staring. They were too drunk to care. They tilted their glasses back, drinking the last of their margaritas, and motioned for the waitress so they could close out their tab. On the way out, they all took a trip to the bathroom.

"We're going toward downtown, but you guys just follow me. I think I know where it is," Lynda said.

"Hey . . . you sure you've never been?" Nikki asked Lynda. Lynda just smiled and kept on walking.

"Bam!" Kevin yelled, throwing down the big joker. "Y'alls asses are set again!"

"Damn, Kevin. Let's let them win one game," Jason said sarcastically.

"Whatever, man, sit your high-yellow ass down," Chris said. "We're only down by 175 and the game isn't over, punk."

"We'll see you guys on the back end of 350," Rick said.

"Is this the last game?" Kevin asked.

"Depends on what time it is," Chris said.

"Why, what time do you have to be home?" Jason asked, trying to start shit.

"Man, please," Chris said. "Be home? Not until after I stop by Renee's for my fix."

"Ohhhhhhhh . . . Okay, you've got Renee jokes now, huh?" Jason asked, sitting up and leaning toward Chris.

"Yeah," Chris said, "I thought that would shut your ass up pretty quick."

"Yeah, he can't stand for anybody to talk about his little Renee," Rick said mockingly. "So, Jay, man, seriously . . . all jokes aside . . . is it going to be hard for you if I pull Renee's key next weekend?" Kevin asked. The room fell silent. He wished he could have taken it back as soon as he said it.

"No. It won't be too hard. Not nearly as hard as my dick will be by the time I get started on Kay!"

"Ohhhhhhhhh, shit," Chris said.

"All right, no fighting up in here!" Rick said.

"Naw, man," Kevin said to Rick. "Don't worry about me . . . I'm a lover, not a fighter," glaring at Jason.

They started the next hand in complete silence.

Finally, Kevin reached out and punched Jason in the shoulder lightly. "C'mon, man, you know I was just fucking with you."

"Whatever," Jason said, trying to keep a stone-cold look on his face.

"I'll probably end up with Lynda's key anyway, so don't worry," Kevin said. Rick spat out his beer unexpectedly and they all started laughing.

"Hey!" Kevin said. "I know what . . . let's go to the CITY."

"Damn, man," Chris said. "You would live in that bitch if you could, huh?"

"Oh, don't try and act like you don't like to go . . . like I'm dragging you there every time. If I didn't know any better I would think you had something going on with that Nefratiti chick."

"Whatever, man, I like her little body, but she ain't got nothing on my Nikki, punk. If Rick will drop me off on the way home, I'll go."

"I would, man, but I really hadn't planned on being out that late. I wanted to come hang and get home in enough time to catch Lynda awake."

"Awww . . . isn't that sweet?" Kevin said.

"Shut the hell up," Rick said. "Maybe next time, man."

"That's cool, man, I could stand to save two hundred dollars anyway," Kevin said.

"Me too," Chris said.

"Yeah, I'm tired as hell," Jason said, yawning.

Rick was glad he had been able to get out of that one with little effort. In the past, it had been pretty difficult. His boys had always pressed and pressed, asking why he was always trying to get in so early. He just told them it was to spend more time with Lynda. They didn't know that he had other plans. He made these plans at least every other month. He couldn't help himself. He had been so lonely at times that he could have just killed himself. The counseling was definitely helping. But like with any bad habit, it would take time to get it out of his system.

It had started one day about two years ago when Lynda was out of town doing a training seminar. Their sex life had been nonexistent for about three months before her departure and he was at one of the lowest points he had ever been in since they had gotten married. The next evening at a business dinner, one of his clients mentioned an escort service he used whenever he was in town. Rick had taken this client out to dinner to celebrate closing a deal they had been working on for six months. The client was talking freely about his wife as well as his "escort honey." He didn't seem to think there was a damn thing wrong with it. Rick laughed when everyone else laughed and went along with the conversation. In his mind, though, he was taking notes.

The next month while Lynda had been traveling on one of her business trips he dialed the number for the first time. He remembered being so nervous that he hung up when he heard the female voice on the other end. About an hour passed before he had the nerve to call again. "Hello," the voice on the other end had said. "How may I help you?" she asked.

"Um . . . hi . . . yes, I, um, I wanted to inquire about an escort possibly?"

"Sure," the young woman said. "I just have a couple of questions I need to ask you first.

"Okay," he said. By the end of the conversation he had it set up to meet his escort at the Marriott Marquis later that evening. The damage was three hundred dollars, but he didn't care. He had gotten there early to check in and have a couple of drinks before the escort would arrive. He was on his second Hennessy and Coke when he heard the knock on the door. He opened the door, not realizing the chain lock was on; he almost took the door off the hinge trying to get it open. For the first thirty minutes they just talked; the escort had been fine with that. The only rule was they couldn't get too personal. All he wanted to do was buy some time before they had to get down to business. He realized that he wasn't looking as forward to the sex as he thought he would be. It was just nice to have someone listening to him. Whether they were really hearing what he was saying or not, it was just what he needed.

They did eventually get down to business. The sex had been different, much different than what he was used to with Lynda. He fucked the escort in ways he had never been able to fuck Lynda. Maybe it was because

she was his wife or just because they had never opened
up to each other that freely. When it was over he
handed the escort four hundred dollars. He couldn't
believe what he had done. Over the next year, he had
four or five more visits with the same escort. Each time
he promised himself it would be the last.

"Let's wrap this thing up, then," he heard Kevin saying as he snapped out of his daydream.

"Yeah, it's been real, fellas," Rick said, standing up
first.

"I'll drop you off, Jason," Chris said.

"Thanks, man."

"Well, you men go home to your women while I
drink up the rest of this beer and eat this pizza," Kevin
said, smiling and rubbing his stomach.

"Thanks for the hospitality, man," Rick said.

"No problem, dog, next month we're doing it at your
crib, right?" Kevin asked Rick.

"Yeah, that's cool," Rick said, putting his coat on. As
he was walking to his car, he was calculating how long it
would take to get to the hotel across town and meet his
escort.

The girls parked in the front since it was so dark.
Renee looked nervous as hell. Kay looked curious as
hell.

"Relax, ladies," Lynda said.

"We're cool," Nikki said, pretending to have it all together.

"Wait," Renee said, grabbing Nikki's coat, keeping

her from going inside. "Are they going to think we're gay?"

"Yeah, I never thought about that," Kay said.

"I guess they will, but who cares?" Lynda said.

"Let's go," Nikki said, walking inside the front door.

"That'll be twenty dollars," the lady behind the window said, busy counting money. They all passed their twenty-dollar bills up to Lynda. She handed the chick the money and the bouncer waved them on toward the entrance to the club. The music was extremely loud and nothing could have prepared them for the naked women swinging around the poles with their legs up in the air.

"Oh, hell no," Renee said to Kay, "I'm outta here." Nikki was laughing.

"Let's just find an empty table and order some drinks," Lynda said.

"That'll calm you down," Nikki said, looking at Renee.

They found a table near the back of the club and took a seat. The DJ was announcing the next dancer. "Coming to the stage we have the African queen of your dreams. She's sensual, she's beautiful . . . Please welcome . . . Nefratitiiiiiiiiiiiiiiiiiiiiiiiiiiiiiiiiiiiiiiiiii," he yelled into the mic. All of the girls' eyes were glued to the stage.

"Damn," Lynda said out loud, "she's so beautiful."

"Yeah," Kay said. "Fine as hell! Damn."

"Chris would like her, I bet," Nikki said, whispering to Kay, who was sitting closest to her. "She's got those long legs."

Nefratiti was on the stage doing her thing. She was working those long legs, which equaled big dollars for her.

"Okay, now she's butt-ass naked," Kay said so all the girls could hear her.

"Yeah, I know," Nikki said. "That's kind of crazy and how in the hell does she make her ass shake like that?" The waitress walked over to take their drink order and said she'd be right back. Right after the waitress walked away a tall dark chick came over in a maid's uniform. She stopped near Renee.

"Can I dance for you ladies?" she asked.

"Dance for who?" Renee said, looking at the rest of her girls.

"Not right now," Lynda said. "Maybe later." She smiled at the woman, who sauntered off to the next table.

"So women get dances from other women here?" Kay asked.

"Even I knew that much," Renee said.

"Well, excuse the hell out of me. I must have missed Strip Club Etiquette 101 in school."

"C'mon, girls . . . try not to be so serious. We're supposed to be enjoying ourselves," Nikki said.

The waitress brought their drinks right on time. They all sipped their drinks in silence, watching as woman after woman graced the stage. Sometimes, they would come up two at a time and dance with each other.

After about an hour or so, Lynda could tell that Kay, Renee, and Nikki were feeling a lot more comfortable. Kay and Renee were moving to the music and Nikki was watching the women, yelling at the stage.

"I want a lap dance," Nikki said, "just so I can say I've had one."

"I'll buy you one," Kay said. "How should I do it?"

"Hell if I know."

"I guess we just find the girl you want and then call her over," Lynda said.

"Okay, well, I want that one," Nikki said, pointing at a tall blond woman who had a neon-green bikini on. She was in the process of finishing up a dance for some guys across the room. When Lynda saw the dancer look over she threw her hand up in the air, trying not to look too anxious. The young woman nodded her head to let them know she would be right over.

"Oh my gosh, I change my mind."

"She's walking over here now," Lynda said.

"Ha, ha . . . it's too late," Renee and Kay said at the same time.

"Shut up," Nikki said, rolling her eyes playfully. When Nikki looked up all she saw was green. The woman was standing right in front of her.

"Can I dance for you ladies?" she said. "My name is Daisy."

"Um, yeah . . . she would like a dance," Kay said, pointing at Nikki. Nikki had a stunned look on her face even though she was smiling.

Daisy straddled Nikki and began her routine. She turned around, facing the stage with her backside facing Nikki, and bent all the way over. Her bare behind was about one and a half inches from Nikki's face. The green thong bikini bottom was almost invisible in the midst of all that ass. Nikki was in total shock. She blindly moved her hand around the table, looking for her drink. Daisy was busy slipping out of her top at this point. That's when Nikki did something that surprised all of her girls. She reached out and ran her hand slowly over Daisy's bare ass. Daisy turned around and smiled. The girls were sitting there with their mouths wide open in sheer surprise.

"Not one stretch mark," Nikki yelled at her girls. "Unbelievable. How do you do it?" she asked Daisy, trying to yell over the music.

"I just don't have them. Some of the other girls here use some kind of cream that works pretty good to cover theirs up."

"Your skin is just beautiful," Nikki said, complimenting Daisy.

Daisy leaned up and whispered in Nikki's ear, "Thank you . . . so is yours."

Nikki was totally embarrassed, knowing that this chick was flirting with her in front of everyone. Renee kept sipping on her drink and was shaking her head from side to side, still not believing she was there. Lynda was too busy watching Nikki's lap dance to hear Kay over the music.

"Do you want one too?" Kay screamed at Lynda.

"Huh?" Lynda said, realizing that Kay was talking to her.

"Oh no. I'm good . . . thanks, Kay. Why don't you get one?"

"No, thanks, I'll be just fine if I *never* get a lap dance."

"I hear that!" Renee said.

Kay was getting up from her chair walking toward the stage.

"Where are you going?" Lynda said.

"I'm going to tip the girls . . . isn't that what you're supposed to do?"

"I'll go with you," Renee said, jumping up. She had wanted to go up there all night but was just too embarrassed. Of course, Kay would beat her to the punch. When the girls came and took their seats, there was a dancer standing near Lynda talking about something. The woman finally walked away.

"What did she want?" Renee asked Lynda.

"She wanted to know if we wanted to go into one of the VIP rooms with her." It hadn't sounded like a bad idea at all to Lynda, but she knew better than to try and convince her crew. It had been enough for them just coming out to the club in the first place.

"What goes on in the VIP room?" Kay and Nikki said.

"Anything money can buy."

"Damn," Kay said, "it's like that, huh?"

"Yup. They do it all in there."

"I need to ask Chris more about these VIP rooms," Nikki said, half joking.

"You ladies ready to go?" Lynda said. "I bet Rick is wondering where my black ass is."

"Yeah, I had fun, though," Nikki said. "Got my first lap dance. I feel like a new woman."

"It was different than what I expected," Renee said. "It really wasn't that bad."

"Yeah, I had a good time myself. The next time me and Kevin are bored I'm going to suggest that we come here and blow his damn mind," Kay said, laughing and smacking Lynda's hand, giving her a high five.

"Me too," Nikki said.

Rick's visit with his escort turned out to be a huge success. Rick had gotten his emotions involved somehow and so did his date. Rick told his escort that it would be his last time scheduling a visit. He felt guilty now that his emotions were starting to get involved. He wasn't ready to end his marriage over this. The only thing he got in response from the escort was "Okay."

Rick hated himself for getting caught up in this. He checked out of the room and headed toward home. He figured Lynda would be sleeping. He would try to make love to her anyway, to forget about what had just happened.

"Hello?" Nikki said as she woke out of a deep sleep.

"Wake up, sleepyhead," Chris said. "I've been trying to call you all morning. You are so late for work right now, Nikki. What time did you get in?"

"I'll call you when I get to work, babe, and explain everything. It was a crazy night."

"No worries, babe," Chris said. "I love you."

"Thanks for waking me. I love you too." Nikki jumped up and flew into the shower. She must have been out of her fucking mind. She had a deadline to meet and she was running late for work. She got to work in record time, which for her meant like twelve minutes. Things didn't turn out to be the disaster she thought they would be, after all. She had forgotten that her deadline had been stretched two days last Friday, giving her until Wednesday morning to finish things up. She was so tired, though. She got up to go into the break room and fix some coffee. There were five boxes of piping-hot Krispy Kreme doughnuts in there that were right on time. She finished fixing her coffee and grabbed two doughnuts, making her way back to her desk. She had had no idea what time she had gotten home, but Chris had been in a deep sleep when she passed out on the bed next to him. She had way too much to drink, but had a really good time with the girls. Those drinks at the CITY really sneaked up on her. She didn't realize how drunk she was until they had gotten up to leave.

Nikki needed to talk to Chris. She felt guilty for getting home so late. Or, was it because she had gotten home after he did? It was a rare occasion that Chris would beat her home if they both happened to be hanging out on the same night. It felt kind of nice to come home and see him sleeping for a change, she had to admit. She picked up the phone to dial his number. He answered on the first ring.

"Hey, baby," Chris said. "I was hoping it would be you."

He was always so sweet, Nikki thought. "I feel like shit, but I'm here, babe."

"That's what you get for trying to hang with the big dogs when you're just a puppy, Nick."

"Whatever," Nikki said, laughing at Chris.

"So what did you guys do?" Chris said. "Did you get that sloppy drunk at Bahama Breeze?"

"Well, we started out there and then decided to go to a strip club."

"Oh, really! I didn't know those Chippendale guys were still around."

"Oh no, we went to one of your spots, it was a women's strip club."

"What? You mean like the CITY?"

"Yup, that's exactly where we went, actually. And believe it or not, I had a blast! After I got used to all the naked women, it wasn't so bad. The first dancer we saw was Nefratiti."

"Nefratiti, huh?" Chris said. He couldn't believe his wife was just sitting there naming off his favorite dancer like it was nothing. "So you're an expert now? How about Daisy?" he said, not expecting her to know that one.

"Yeah, the blond one? Kay bought me a lap dance from her."

"What? No way. You're tripping me out. Why did you guys go there anyway?"

"I don't know," Nikki said, feeling like she was being scolded. "Just something new to do. We wanted to see what the big deal was. To see why you guys go so much, I guess."

"Oh!" Chris said. "Cool . . . Well, I need to go finish some work."

He sounded mad, Nikki thought. Maybe he thought they should have gone together first or something. She didn't know and once he said he needed to go it wasn't the time to talk about it.

"All right, Chris," Nikki said. "Have a good day. I'll talk to you later."

"Later," Chris said.

She hung up the phone, not knowing why he sounded so cold at the end of the conversation. She needed to know what it was. Against her instincts she picked up the phone and dialed his work number again. She knew that the double ring meant she would get his voice mail, so she left a message. "Hi, babe, I'm not sure why you sounded funny before we hung up, but I feel like we need to talk. I'll make reservations at the Spanish Fly in Buckhead for seven-thirty. I'll see you then. I love you."

Six

Tick . . . Tock

Kevin was so nervous to finally be getting the results back. Most of his players had taken their final exams the previous week and their final grades were coming out today. It was almost time for them to leave for winter break. There were two students in particular that he was concerned about. Greg and Charley were both on academic probation and wouldn't touch the field the next season if their grades weren't good enough. He had put in overtime with these two boys, knowing that they wouldn't disappoint him. Endless nights in the library and in their dorms he spent going over what tutors had already gone over with them. He wanted to see them play. More importantly, he wanted to see them graduate. He was sitting in his office when his door opened wide enough for him to see his secretary's head poking in.

"The dean is here to see you, Kevin," Shelly said, looking scared.

"Dean Carter?" Kevin said, confused.

"Yes."

"Okay, give me two seconds and then send him in."

Dean Carter was a short, scrawny white man who held the futures of many of his players in the palms of his hands. He loved to see them go down; felt as if they were too privileged in the first place. He was probably the kid who never got picked for a team or who got picked last when he was growing up.

"Dean Carter?" Kevin said, walking from behind his desk to shake the dean's hand.

"Hello, Kevin, long time no see."

"Yes, sir, that's a good thing as far as I'm concerned."

"I have some bad news," Dean Carter said.

No shit, Kevin thought.

"It has been brought to my attention that two of your players were caught cheating in McGregor's Calculus Two class."

"I don't believe what I'm hearing." That had always been his immediate response to Carter's allegations even though he knew some of them were true. "Who might these two kids be?"

"Well, it looks like it was Greg Wilson and Charley Rollins. From what I've been told, another student in the class reported that they were talking during the final exam and even passed a sheet of paper during the test. This type of behavior is unacceptable and will not be tolerated. I suggest that you sit those hoodlums down and have a long talk with them about integrity," Carter said, still standing.

"Have a seat, Dean Carter. Let me start by saying this. As far as I'm concerned they didn't do it unless the student who reported it is willing to give his or her statement in front of Greg and Charley as procedure goes. Secondly, you're the hoodlum. You're the one who pimps these boys for everything they have and reaps the benefits of every championship they win or bowl invite that they get. So, if you don't mind, I'm careful about the company I keep and I'd appreciate it if you would get out of my office. No pimps . . . no hoodlums . . . you must not have seen my office rules. They're posted on the outside of my door. Read them on the way out, Carter!" Kevin said, infuriated.

He was pissed with Greg and Charley, but he was more upset with this son of a bitch who didn't know the first thing about being a black college athlete at a white university.

Kevin sat back down and put his head in his hands; he was ready to go home. He didn't want to see anyone. How was he supposed to tell the head coach about this shit? It was his job to keep the boys in line, so to speak. The next season would be shot unless the head coach could work a deal with Carter. And, based on the things Kevin had said to Carter, he doubted it would be possible.

Kevin called and left Greg and Charley a message on their dorm room answering machine. They were roommates. He simply told them that he needed to see them first thing the next morning in his office. Kevin really needed to talk to Kay at that moment. He was tired and needed someone to listen to him vent and assure him things would work out.

Jason was in one of his moods again, and for once Renee didn't want to be bothered. He hadn't called her in two days, nor was he returning any of her calls. This was starting to happen more often and she was getting tired of it. If he had a problem, he needed to discuss it with her. The guessing games had to end, she thought. It really concerned her when he got so down and out. But there was nothing she could do to console him. His immediate reaction to her attempts was to shut her out completely. The more she tried, the further away he seemed to withdraw. There had to be something more. She felt as if he had started to tell her on several occasions and then stopped himself. She never pressed him to go further, although she was dying to know what it was that drove him into these moods of depression. Either way, the least he could do was call, she figured. He knew she would worry. She made a conscious decision to go about her day without worrying herself sick over it this time. If he didn't want to call, there was nothing she could do about it. But she was definitely going to tell him about himself when she did talk to him. Her phone rang.

"Hello?"

"Hey, sis."

"Hi, Kay, what's up?" Renee said, sounding way too excited. She was really happy to hear her sister's voice on the other end. She didn't realize how Jason's drama had started to consume her every thought.

"I need to talk to you. It's important. Can we meet?"

"Yeah, I can meet you tonight. How about if we meet at your place at six-thirty and just take one car?" Renee said, finalizing the plans.

"That's perfect. See you then. Love ya!"

"All right then . . . love you too, Kay," Renee said, smiling. It had been a long time since she had said those words to her sister. She hoped that tonight would allow them to put some things behind them and get back on track. She wanted their relationship to get better.

"Damn," Renee said, looking at her watch. It was already five o'clock. She would leave around five forty-five so she could get to Kay's in plenty of time. She couldn't wait to eat dinner. They were going to a quiet spot in Midtown to catch a bite and talk. Renee was looking forward to it.

When Renee hung up the phone she realized that her message light was on. She was hoping Jason had tried to call. She was pretty proud of herself, though. Finally, she had not given in to his latest episode and he had decided to call her instead. It was a big step for her. She loved Jason so much that she found herself catering to his every need. It was beginning to take its toll on her.

She could not believe her ears when she finally dialed her phone code to access her messages. Jason had left her a very disturbing message. She was trying to keep her composure, but she couldn't. He didn't sound like himself and he was saying some very awful things. The most offensive thing he had said was that she was a selfish bitch and that he couldn't care less about her or the wedding they were planning for next year. As far as he was concerned, Jason said, she could consider it canceled. He was apparently upset that she didn't hunt him down this time to see what had been troubling him. At some point in the message, it was hard to hear him since he was yelling and sounding as if he was even crying. He was saying that he hated women and that he had thought Renee was different. He said he needed time to think and that he would be back in town the following day and that she shouldn't try to contact him. By the end of the message he was already apologizing for his behavior.

She was so scared. This was the worst he had ever

been. He'd never called her a bitch before; she didn't know what to do. She had no idea where he was going or when to expect his next call. The tears were flowing heavily at this point; he was ruining everything. She was looking so forward to the key party on Saturday, and now with Jason's dramas she didn't know what they would do. She gathered her belongings and told her boss she had a family emergency and needed to leave for the day. She got in her car and headed toward Kay's apartment. It was comforting to know that Kay would be there for her to talk to about what had happened. All she wanted was for Jason to let her help him. For all it was worth, she was a good listener. Maybe she could at least give him good advice about what was troubling him. She had noticed that the anxiety attacks were coming more often and were even more extreme. Seeing him that way was not easy, and anything she could do to help she was willing to do. She pulled up in front of Kay's place and realized she wasn't there yet. Renee had a key and decided to go on up anyway and just relax until Kay got home.

Kevin declared today as his worst day since he had started coaching. Once Coach Randall found out that the guys had been accused of cheating he proceeded to tear Kevin a new asshole. He was upset mostly because he knew the next season would be a complete wash without the two star players. Kevin had taken the verbal abuse without arguing with Randall at all. He understood Randall's position and knew things wouldn't stay so heated after Randall had some time to think. He left Randall's office and headed straight for the parking lot. He was out of there for the day. He just wanted to go home and lie in Kay's lap. Unfortunately, she had plans with Renee and wasn't going to be home until later that evening. He had a date with six bottles of Icehouse beer, so he didn't really mind. He couldn't wait to get home and drink his face off. He figured he would go ahead and try to catch Kay before she and Renee left for dinner. He wanted to down a couple brews first, though, just to calm him a bit.

While he lay on the couch he had an epiphany of sorts. Kevin suddenly realized that the key party was only days away. It had seemed like an eternity since they had all discussed it. He was almost looking forward to it. Kay had been talking about it quite a bit it in the last month and seemed a lot more secure with things. The last thing he wanted was for some stupid party to destroy their relationship. He loved her very much. He had thought about what would happen if he were to pull Renee's key. He didn't allow himself to think about it too often or for too long. There was something about Renee that still moved him and he couldn't deny it. He wasn't even sure if he wanted to.

Kevin got into the house and immediately went to the fridge to grab a cold one. He downed it before he finished checking the messages. There was one from Kay saying she loved him and that she was glad she had asked for his advice about whether or not she should have this talk with Renee. He had told her that it wasn't a bad idea to squash the past so they could move forward. He went and grabbed his second beer and cut the radio on. Maxwell was singing his ass off to some new song he had out. That brother could blow, Kevin said to himself. He lay back and let his body sink into his couch. It welcomed him with open arms. He dialed Kay's number and was glad to hear her pick up.

"Hello."

"Hey, baby," Kevin said. "Can I come over there and lick you all over?"

"Um, hello, who is this?"

"So you wanna play hard to get, huh, Kay? I just want to put my hands on that ass of yours and put my—"

"Kevin!" Renee yelled, embarrassed.

"Oh, shit," he said, "Renee?"

"Yes, it's me," Renee said, laughing in an attempt to lighten the situation up.

"I am soooooooooo sorry."

"No problem, I needed a laugh anyway."

"I guess Kay isn't home yet?"

"No, I'm waiting on her now so we can go get something to eat. So, how are you, Kevin? It's been a while since I've talked to you."

"Actually, Renee, I'm having the *worst* day of my life."

"Why, what happened?"

Kevin was on his fourth beer. He just wanted to talk and have someone listen. Kay had always been really good at that. He was learning now that Renee was equally as good. She was a really genuine person and one of the nicest people he had ever met, he thought.

"Renee, do you remember the day we met?" he asked, not knowing where the words were coming from.

"Yes, at Club 112."

"Yeah, well, ever since that day, I haven't been able to forget about you." There was complete silence on the other end.

"Listen, Renee, I'm not trying to create a problem here and I don't want to make you feel uncomfortable either, I just had to get it off my chest. I've never really stopped thinking about you. I mean, don't get me wrong here, I love your sister," he continued. "But for some reason you just make me want to hand you my paycheck and give you the world."

"I don't know what to say," Renee said. "I remember the day we played spin the bottle and I will admit that it was a great moment in there with you, but I've always loved you for treating my sister so good. You're the best thing that's ever happened to her."

"And you're the best thing that's ever happened to *me*," Kevin said. "I'm not asking you to respond in any way, I just had to let you know, and since I'm sitting here drinking my ass off and you happened to answer the phone, I figured this was as good a time as any."

"Oh, so you're drunk, huh? That's what this is about."

"No, I'm not drunk yet, but I'm getting there and I'll make a point to get drunk now that I've completely embarrassed myself." They both laughed.

"Kevin, I'm flattered, I really am, but I . . ." Renee couldn't finish her sentence. She had started to cry. "Sometimes I wish things had been different too, circumstances, you know," she continued.

"Are you crying? Renee, what's wrong?" he said, sitting up in his chair.

"It's just . . . me and Jason are having some problems, that's all. I don't think I can help him and I don't know what to do about it anymore."

"Talk to me, what's happening with Jay?"

The line beeped.

"Hold on, Kevin," Renee said, clicking over to the other line. "Hello?" she said, trying to cover up the fact that she was crying. It was Kay.

"I'll be there in ten minutes, sis," Kay said. "I'm starving, so be ready to roll, okay?"

"All right, sis, see you in a minute," Renee said.

"Are you on the other line?" Kay said.

"Um, yeah, just hurry up and get here so we can go," Renee said, dodging the question. She clicked back over.

"That was Kay," Renee said, bringing the conversation right back to where it had begun.

"Oh, cool," he said. "Maybe I should let you go."

"Yeah, Kevin, Kay will be here soon."

"Well, Rey, I'm always here for you if you just want to talk . . . and I mean about anything. It kills me to see you sad!"

"Thanks, Kevin, you're so sweet."

"All right, well I'll let you go now," Kevin said, not wanting to hang up. "Talk to you later . . . love you . . . I mean see you later, Renee . . . ohhh, damn . . ." Kevin said, embarrassed at his admission.

"Love you too, Kevin," Renee said, smiling, gleaming actually, for the first time all day.

Nikki got to the Spanish Fly in just enough time to see Chris pull up to the valet and hop out of his car. She had a nice window seat and he had seen her too. He flashed that charming smile of his to let her know that things were okay between them.

"Hi, honey," Nikki said, standing on her tiptoes as always to hug her six-foot-four hunk of a man.

"Hey, babe," Chris said, kissing her forehead. They both took their seats.

"I already ordered us drinks and an appetizer," Nikki said, smiling at Chris.

"Cool. So are you feeling better, baby?" he asked, running his hand down the side of her face.

"Much better."

"So, what made you decide on dinner?"

"Mainly because you seemed mad at me this morning when I talked to you."

"Who, me?" Chris asked, pretending not to know what she was talking about.

"Yeah, you," Nikki said, reaching over the table to poke him in the chest.

He grabbed her finger before she could pull her hand back and kissed it. "I wasn't mad, baby, I think I was just a little jealous. That's all that was."

"Jealous of what, Chris?"

"Well, I just wasn't expecting you to say you'd been to the CITY, and then on top of that you knew more of the dancers' names than I did. Plus, you got home really late and I just wasn't used to being home waiting up for you. It just felt like the roles had been reversed a bit. I'm sorry for being so lame."

"That's all? You had me thinking I was in trouble all day, and that's it? Well, I wanted to meet you tonight because I wanted to make some things clear between us, just make sure we're on the same page, so to speak. I know the fact that the key party is this weekend has a lot to do with your reaction to my little rendezvous the other night, babe. Chris, I've always prided myself on how in touch we are with each other, you know. . . . I think the reason our relationship has been so good is that we have a great deal of respect for one another in every facet of our lives. You've never tried to change me and I've never attempted to make changes in you. Instead, I think we've chosen to embrace those things about the other person that didn't make us so comfortable. I wanted you to come here tonight to tell you that I'll call the key party off if you want me to. I know that for the most part you could take it or leave it and that you're only really doing it because you know I wanted to."

"Are you serious, Nikki?" Chris said, adjusting in his chair. "I can't believe you'd be willing to do that . . . It means a lot to me knowing that you would make that sacrifice and disappoint all of your friends for me, babe. But unfortunately, I'm not letting you off that easy. You might as well get used to the idea that one of your girls is going to get a taste of your Prince Charming," he said, licking his lips.

"Shut up, Chris," Nikki said, laughing. "Whatever, don't try and act like you're not worried about me getting a taste. Because I know you are."

"It's all good, babe," Chris said. "You don't have to cancel anything, the key party is just that, a party. I know we'll come through this just fine. I love you, Nikki."

"I know you do," Nikki said.

Lynda and Rick were at home relaxing on the couch watching TV when they heard a loud bang on the door. Lynda jumped up, startled at the loud noise.

"Who the hell could that be?" Rick said.

"I'm not expecting anyone," Lynda said. Lynda got off Rick's lap so he could get up and answer the door.

"Who is it?" Rick said.

"It's me, man, open the door," the voice said. "It's Jason."

Lynda and Rick were a little perturbed. Rick opened the door and the smell of brandy hit him like a ton of bricks.

"Whoa, partner, hang on just a minute," Rick said as he closed the door, leaving Jason standing outside.

"Lynda, go upstairs for a minute, would you? Until I figure out what's going on with him."

"All right, baby, is everything okay?"

"I don't know, just go upstairs."

Rick went back to the foyer and opened the door, letting Jason in. He was staggering and smelled terrible. His clothes were wrinkled and had obviously been worn a couple of days in a row. He looked like he hadn't shaved in forever. Jason walked toward Rick's living room and took a seat on the couch.

"So what's up, man?" Jason asked as if there was nothing out of the ordinary going on.

"No, what's up with *you*, man?"

"Not much. I'm just a little tired, that's all."

"Tired? Where are you coming from?"

"A hotel over on Spring Street. Isn't that funny? I just checked out and I can't even remember the name of it," Jason said with a stupid grin on his face.

"What's going on, Jason? You look like hell."

"Yeah, well, that's where I told Renee she could go too. Straight to hell!"

Before Rick could interrupt to ask questions, Jason was already talking as if Rick wasn't even there.

"I told her that she was a bitch and that I hated her and that she could throw that fucking ring away. I told her that I didn't think I would ever measure up to being the man she needed or wanted."

"Jason!" Rick yelled to get his attention. "Did you really say those things to Renee?"

"Nah, I left them on her answering machine."

"What the hell is up with you, Jason? How could you say those things to her, man?" Rick asked, looking stunned. "Are you trying to lose her forever?"

"I know, man," Jason said, holding his head between both his hands. "I've really messed up this time."

"What can I do to help, Jason? Anything?"

"I just feel lost, man. I was scared I might do something crazy and I didn't want to be alone. I just didn't want to be alone, man," Jason repeated, starting to cry. "I just want to find Renee and tell her I'm sorry before it's too late."

"Have you called her?"

"No, every time I pick up the phone and get ready to dial her number my stomach starts turning."

"Well, that's that liquor doing the flips," Rick said. They both laughed a bit. "Listen, man, get your shit together and call the girl."

"Okay, man, let me use your phone."

"All right. But first you need to go in the bathroom and get yourself in order. I'll get the phone for you." As Rick got up to get the phone in the kitchen he heard scurrying steps at the top of the stairs. He laughed to himself at Lynda's attempt to hurry back to the bedroom so she wouldn't be caught eavesdropping.

Jason came out of the bathroom looking more like himself, Rick thought. Rick had heard by way of Lynda that Jason and Renee's relationship was a rocky one the majority of the time. In fact, Lynda had given him the impression on several occasions that things between Jason and Renee were downright dysfunctional. Of course, Jason was the source of most, if not all, of the problem, from what Rick could tell. Plus, Renee was just too sweet to be causing all the ruckus between the two of them.

"Listen," Rick said, putting his hand on Jason's shoulder. "I don't know what's causing you the stress you've been under lately or what sets you off from time to time in general, but I think you need some help, man. Now I know you did not come here for a lecture, but I can't let you go on thinking it's okay to continue riding this emotional roller coaster you've been on for the past year. And it's definitely not fair to force Renee to join you on the ride."

"So you think she's giving up on me, huh?" Jason said, standing up.

Rick could see the veins in Jason's jaw, he was gritting his teeth so hard. He started pacing the floor . . . back and forth. Rick had to admit that he was a little nervous; he hoped he wasn't going to have to bust Jason's ass up in there. He didn't play that temper tantrum . . . blame-it-on-the-liquor bullshit. He would kick Jason's ass with no hesitation if he started acting up in his crib.

"What have you heard?" Jason said. "Tell me. Go ahead and just tell me!"

"This is what I'm talking about," Rick said. "No one said anything about Renee giving up on you. You're not listening to me! You need to get a handle on your temper . . . and I mean now, man. My wife is upstairs and I won't have you up in here acting a damn fool. So, get it together now or get the fuck out."

Jason sat down on the couch and let it all go. "I'm so sorry, man. I didn't mean any disrespect. I have so much going on right now and I know I'm making things worse by turning on the people who are trying to help. I just feel like I've taken it too far with Renee . . . too far for her to forgive me."

"All you need to do is leave her a message and let her know you need to talk to her. Explain that you know you went too far and that you are willing to do whatever you have to do to make it up to her. Whatever you say, you better mean it and you better make it count. You might want to say the important shit up front too, in case she deletes the message without listening to the entire thing."

Jason shook his head without uttering a word. He knew Rick was right. He took the phone into the dining room and made the call.

"I'll drive," Kay said hurrying into the house. "Let me go to the bathroom really quick and we can roll, sis."

Renee felt guilty as soon as she saw Kay walk through the door. Not only had she been completely caught off guard by the things that Kevin had told her, but it had almost been comforting in her time of turmoil with Jason.

"Hey," Renee yelled, "what are you doing in there? I know you're not changing clothes. This isn't some runway show. Let's just go eat please, I'm starving."

"I'm coming, I'm coming," Kay said, coming out of the bedroom, having changed into a little denim outfit and slipping on a pair of beige boots.

Renee rolled her eyes. "Can we go now, Tyra?" she said jokingly.

"Yeah, let's go," Kay said, smiling.

It only took twenty minutes to get to the restaurant. This was their first time going there together. Oddly enough, about a year ago they had realized that it was a favorite restaurant for the both of them. The food was delicious and inexpensive, a combination they just couldn't beat. They parked in a lot across from the restaurant and headed toward the main entrance. It was pretty empty when they walked in. The after-work rush hadn't made it there yet.

"Hi," Kay said to the woman standing behind the podium. "I have reservations for two, last name Campbell."

"Right this way," she said, waving them on toward the middle of the restaurant. It was extremely dim inside, lit by candlelight. There were little tea candles on each table. It was obvious that the restaurant used to be a house. Their table ended up being in what seemed to have been the living room.

"I'll be right back to take your drink order."

"Actually," Kay said, "just bring two glasses of Chateau St. Michelle please."

"So, big sister," Renee said, taking off her coat. "What's the deal? What did you want to talk to me about?"

"Man, you don't waste time, do you?"

"Well, I'm a little anxious, you know, always have been."

"I guess I just wanted to turn over a new leaf, Renee. This year is coming to an end in like three months and I want to make some things right that have been wrong for a long time. When Daddy came to visit, it really put some things in perspective for me. For the first time in forever, I have accepted that Mom is gone and that we're all each other has. I don't want to live another day missing out on having a better relationship with my twin sister."

Renee was very surprised. She was amazed at Kay's display of maturity and proud of her older sister.

"Kay, I—"

"Let me finish, Renee. Growing up I wanted to be you so bad."

"Be me?" Renee asked with a shocked look on her face.

"Yeah, everyone always had this, I don't know, this respect for you. It had a lot to do with the way you carried yourself, I guess. But for whatever reason you've always been taken seriously and that's something I didn't always have growing up. Being twins was hellish for me coming up in high school. You were valedictorian and I was captain of the cheerleading team. Don't get me wrong, I wouldn't change those years, but I just wish I had taken life a little more seriously. I want us to spend more time together from now on. We used to be so tight when we were younger. In spite of all our differences we always had each other's back. I just want to get back to that feeling. I want you to be proud of me, Renee."

"I *am* proud of you, Kay. You're my big sister. Believe it or not, I used to wish I could be more like you. You were so outgoing in high school. Most popular, best dressed, among other accolades. Yeah, I was smart, but so were you. I'm glad you took the initiative to get us back on track. I miss the way things used to be, too."

"The other thing I wanted to tell you," Kay said, "has to do with Kevin."

"What about him?" Renee asked, a little nervous, not knowing where Kay was going with this.

"Well, the key party is in two days and for a while I wasn't too happy about Kevin and me participating."

"No way," Renee said. "Not you, the chance taker, Miss Risky Business herself."

"It was because of you."

"Me? What do I have to do with anything?"

"I know you have no idea about this, but it took me a long time to get over what happened back in the day when we played spin the bottle. I was so jealous of the fact that Kevin was so turned on by you. But I had to ask myself, 'Who wouldn't be?' You're smart, you're sweet, you're beautiful, and you look just like me . . . ha, ha. At first, I wanted to tell Kevin that if he ended up with your key he had to forfeit the whole thing. But I've totally changed my mind. I'm okay with things no matter what. I know that Kevin loves me and that even if he does pull your key, I'm confident now that it doesn't go any deeper than that."

Renee wanted to yell on the inside. She was replaying the conversation she and Kevin had shared just thirty minutes earlier.

"Wow! It looks like you've really come to terms with a lot of different things. I'm glad you feel better about things and I'm definitely willing to do my part to get our relationship moving in a more positive direction. I wish I could say the same for me and Jason," Renee said, looking down. "I don't know what's going to happen with us."

"I thought you said Jason would be cool with this. What's going on? Is he going through one of his rough times again?"

"I guess so, Kay. I didn't want to say this in front of Lynda and Nikki, but honestly I don't really know what the problem is. He just builds this wall up around him and refuses to let anybody in. I try to get him to open up, but he just clams up even tighter. I just can't take it anymore," Renee said, beginning to cry. "It's so stressful at times and I find myself getting lost in the midst of all the chaos."

"Is his temper any better?"

"Um, no. Just today he left me a real foul message at work. I'm too embarrassed to even repeat what he said."

"Now listen. I've wanted to tell you this for quite some time but didn't know how. I just don't think Jason is the right guy for you. I mean, don't get me wrong, I love Jason and he's a real nice successful guy. But for whatever reason, he's allowing his past, a past that he won't even share with you, to ruin your future with him. I just hate to see you so stressed out all the time over Jason's bullshit. You guys are supposed to be getting married next year and he can't even tell you why he loses his temper on a regular basis."

"I know," Renee said.

"I just wish you could find someone like . . . I guess more like Kevin. You deserve someone who is going to love you unconditionally and bring less drama to the table. I'm surprised Jason hasn't ever hauled off and hit you by now or something."

"Yeah," Renee said, wiping her eyes, looking down at her plate.

"Wait a minute. Look at me, Renee!" Kay said, looking her twin sister directly in her eyes. "Has Jason ever hit you?"

"No," Renee said, with tears flowing from her eyes uncontrollably. "I mean, he's yelled at me before, but I used to ignore it and write it off as him being stressed out over a case he was working on or something."

"I asked you if Jason's ever *hit* you," Kay repeated.

"I know what you asked me," Renee said getting angry. "What difference does it make? Jason is *my* problem," Renee said jabbing herself in the chest with her index finger over and over again.

"What? Am I hearing you say that this motherfucker has put his hands on you before?" Kay pulled her cell phone out of her purse. "I'm calling Kevin," she said, dialing on the keypad.

Renee grabbed the phone and put it in her lap. She began to tell Kay what happened.

"It was nothing major," Renee said, reflecting on a situation that had occurred early in her and Jason's relationship. "We had come home from a night out eating dinner and catching a movie. We were both really tired and went to bed as soon as we got back to his place."

Renee paused for what seemed like hours, Kay thought. She was on the edge of her seat waiting to hear more about what Jason had done to her sister.

"About two o'clock that morning I was in the mood, I guess you can say, and I was trying to wake Jason up to get him there too. I kept whispering in his ear, just asking him to make love to me. I think it was the third time I leaned up to whisper that it happened. Before I could finish the sentence he shot straight up in bed and yelled out that he couldn't take it anymore . . . that he *wouldn't* take it anymore. I thought he was talking in his sleep, so I leaned over close to him to shake him awake and he backhanded me, sending me sprawling out on the floor. I couldn't believe what had happened. I lay on the carpet of his bedroom next to his bed for about five minutes holding the side of my face. When he realized what he had done he jumped out of bed and helped me up off the floor. He apologized profusely and said he was having a nightmare and didn't realize it was me talking to him. He begged me to forgive him and never to mention it to anyone.

"I know he didn't mean to do it and nothing like that has happened since then. You have to believe me, Kay."

"I do believe you. You have nothing to be ashamed

of. Jason needs help. He needs his ass kicked too, but that's another story. I know you love him, Renee, but if you really want to marry this guy you can't pretend that he doesn't have some real serious problems."

"You're right. I know you're right. I'm going to talk to him. I've just been avoiding it, you know. It's not easy."

"I know it's not. I'll help you, though. We'll get through this together," Kay said, reaching across the table, hugging her sister close. "It's going to be okay. I promise. I don't know about you, sis, but my heart feels lighter since we've had this talk."

"Yeah, you just happened to ask me to come here at a time when I really needed someone to talk to."

"Just try to put all this behind you until this weekend is over. So what about the key party? Do you think that you and Jason can handle this?"

"I don't know, Kay, but I want to do it. I can't explain it, but I really want to do it. So I'm going to try and take your advice and put all of this behind me for now. Maybe this is what Jason and I need. Some excitement. Maybe he needs to see how it feels for me to be with another man. Maybe then he'll start acting right. I don't know, all I know is that I'm looking forward to the key party . . . to some fun."

"But is Jason going to be okay having sex with someone else? Is he going to be able to participate with your relationship being so rocky right now?"

"As long as I know what I have to do to go forward in this relationship with Jason I'll be fine."

"I'm sure Jason is probably looking forward to the party, isn't he?"

"Well, I think I may have talked him into it. I think he's only doing it because I want to. I just need to talk to him to know that we're going to be okay, that's all. After that, I can start focusing on the important things like who I want to pull my key," Renee said, giggling and wiping tears from her eyes.

"Ha, ha, you're crazy, sis."

"Hey, I thought you were the crazy twin," Renee said, smiling.

Seven

Residence Inn

Nikki pulled up to the hotel around six o'clock. The reservation was in her name and she had planned to get there before everyone to do a little decorating and get things together for the party. She went ahead and checked in at the front desk and then headed toward the room to get settled in.

"Thanks," she told the front desk clerk, smiling.

"Sure," the clerk said, "enjoy yourself!"

"I plan to."

Nikki took the elevator up to the seventh floor and started looking for room 722. She slipped the key card in the door and pushed it open with her shoulder when the green light came on. She hurried inside the door and dropped the bags she was holding on the couch. The suite had turned out to be even roomier than she expected; the kitchen and the living room area were especially big. That was perfect. They would need plenty of room to move around. She couldn't believe it was finally time for the key party. She was thinking back to when this whole thing was just a thought in her head. She was sure it was all going to be fine. At least, she hoped it would. Everyone had made an adult decision and consented to participate. She hoped they had all thought about the extent of what was going to happen later that night.

Nikki expected Chris to get there soon. He said he would come and help her get things set up as soon as he could get home from the gym and shower. She turned the TV on to MTV and ended up catching the end of the *Real World Marathon.* She had to admit that those shows had sucked her in on several occasions. This particular episode was one where the most dysfunctional one in the group was about to get kicked out of the house. Nikki's favorite character was the skinny black guy named Tek. He was so laid-back and just liked to have a good time. She loved him. He was going off on one of the girls for throwing some glasses up against the wall and breaking them.

Nikki jumped up when she heard a knock on the door. She ran over to it and asked, "Who is it?" Looking out the peephole, she could see only a fingerprint covering the hole. "Lynda?"

"Yeah, open up, Nikki."

Nikki was so glad Lynda had gotten there. She opened the door and let her in.

"I'm glad you're here," Nikki said, helping Lynda take off her coat.

"Me too, girl, why is it so quiet in here? This is supposed to be a party, isn't it?"

"You're right," Nikki said, turning the channel to BET, looking for some good videos to add music in the background. "Chris has the CD player, so we'll have to wait on him to play our own music."

"Please tell me you brought your Maxwell CD? I loooooooooove him," Lynda said.

"You know, I've got you. I brought that and I brought Lil' Kim," Nikki said, giving Lynda a high five.

"All right, Lynda. Help me get all of this food unpacked and let's make some drinks."

"I'm so glad we're friends," Lynda said, looking at Nikki.

"Me too. You're my best friend, girl, my homey, my ace, my ace boon coon," Nikki said, laughing.

"Yup, always have been . . . always will be. Now what do you want to drink?" Lynda asked, looking through the grocery bags. "We have wine, Absolut, OJ, cranberry juice, tonic, and Hennessy," she said as she set each bottle on the countertop. "I'm having some Absolut with OJ and cranberry juice."

"Make me one too, then," Nikki said.

"Is that 'I Wanna Rock with You' by Michael Jackson I hear?" Lynda said, walking into the living room where the TV was.

"Yeah," Nikki yelled from the kitchen, "they're doing a two-hour-long tribute to him. Turn that shit up! That will do until Chris and Kevin bring the music."

"So, what's the deal with Jason and Renee?" Lynda asked. "You know he brought his crazy ass to our crib the other day looking wrecked."

"I know, Chris told me. As far as I know from talking to Kay, they just had a really big argument, maybe the biggest ever. Kay said that when she and Renee went to dinner the other night Renee admitted that they had been having serious problems but nothing that couldn't be worked out. Yesterday when I talked to Kay and asked how things were she said it was good for now and that they would both definitely be at the party. She said they had patched things up for now, anyway."

"Damn," Lynda, said. "Is he crazy or what? I mean seriously, I've seen all the Oprah shows and even the ones Queen Latifah has about the children of interracial parents and how they can end up more screwed up than the rest of us, but this boy seems to have a real fucking problem. He flies off the handle at the drop of a dime, from what Rick tells me. I just hope he doesn't pull my key," Lynda said.

"I will have to admit that I don't mind if he pulls mine. He's cute as hell to me."

"Yeah, but he can keep that temper and the drama that goes with it," Lynda said.

"I didn't say I'd marry him," Nikki said, "just screw him." They both started laughing and raised their glasses in the air to toast.

"Now, Kevin is the one with the big dick," Lynda said. "I would put my last damn dollar on that dick."

"It can't be bigger than Chris's," Nikki said. "I learned that a long time ago. Tall men are always hung, or at least eight out of ten tall men are."

"Yeah, but Kevin is built, I mean look at those broad shoulders and that tight ass, *damn*. Pass me those wings so I can put them on this platter."

There was a knock at the door and you could clearly hear women talking and laughing on the other side. Lynda got up to answer it.

"Who is it?"

"Us," Kay and Renee said at the same time.

"Did you guys come in separate cars?" Lynda asked, opening the door.

"Yeah, we know the rules," Renee said, smiling at Lynda.

"Good," Lynda said, "'cause you will be walking home if you're waiting on me to give you a ride somewhere."

"Whatever," Kay said, walking in and getting settled immediately.

"Kevin and Jason should be here in a minute. We talked to them before we left home," Kay said.

"Cool," Nikki said.

"So what's been up, ladies?" Nikki asked, stuffing some cheese and a cracker in her mouth.

"This key party is what's been up," Renee said. "I haven't been able to sleep all week. I mean, it's good nervous energy that's keeping me up, I guess. I just can't believe I'm doing this."

"What?" Nikki said. "Don't look at me. I just suggested the party, and you guys jumped in headfirst like *what!* You guys are the crazy ones, I just try to keep you entertained," she said, smiling.

"Pass me some food," Kay said, "I'm starving!"

There was another knock on the door.

"Get the door please," Nikki said, yelling from the kitchen. Kay, Renee, and Lynda had walked into the living room to find something else on TV.

"I'll get it!" Renee yelled. She was dancing toward the door to a new song that had just come out by DMX.

"It's our men," Renee said as she turned around smiling at Kay and Lynda.

"Good," Lynda said, "we need them to get this thing started."

"Wasssuppp? Wasssuppp? Wasssupppp?" Kevin said.

Kay ran over and gave him a hug and a kiss. Jason and Renee were hugging in the middle of the doorway, blocking the entrance. Right then Chris and Rick walked up right behind them, suddenly appearing in the hallway. Lynda's eyes lit up as if she had seen the puppy she wanted in a pet store window. "Move please," she said, nudging Jason and Renee out of the way to get to Rick.

"Damn," Chris said, walking in, "y'all got my baby all in here slaving by herself." He walked over and grabbed Nikki from behind, whispering, "I'm here, baby." He was making baby faces and kissing Nikki all over her cheeks.

"Well, thank you, baby," Nikki said, giving him a kiss.

"Now make me something to eat and pass me one of those beers we brought," Chris said, slapping Nikki on the behind.

"Ouch," she said as they both started laughing.

"No, seriously, what do you need help with?" Chris asked.

"Ohhh, could you go get the music set up for me so we can get everyone in the party mood? I'm pretty much done with the food. I just have to put the platters out on the table."

"Okay, I'll get the music. Any special requests?" Chris asked, looking back as he walked toward the living room from the kitchen.

"Yeah, play some Maxwell, please."

"You got it, babe," Chris said, giving Nikki a cheesy wink.

"All right, everyone," Nikki said, walking into the living room, "the food is ready. We have wings, cheese and crackers, all kinds of fruit, plenty of liquor, and a chocolate surprise for later chilling in the fridge."

"Let's eat!" Kevin yelled.

"Okay, anybody want a drink while I'm up?" Nikki said, heading back into the kitchen.

"Yeah, Nikki, I want something strong," Kay said.

"Like what? Vodka and cranberry?"

"No, no, no, that's my usual and this isn't the usual night. I want a vodka tonic on the rocks," Kay said.

"Damn," Lynda said, "go head with your bad self."

"Yup, I'm gonna drink my ass off tonight," Kay told them. "I might just drink all three of you ladies under the table."

"Right," Lynda said. "I don't think they make tables with legs high enough for that, homegirl."

Later, Jason and Kay were in the dining room area getting down to some hip-hop song Chris was playing. Kevin and Renee were in there jamming too. Renee was being pretty conservative with her dancing; meanwhile, Kay was all up on Jason's shit in the dining room area. Rick and Lynda were sitting near each other talking and sipping on their drinks. Nikki hadn't even noticed before but the fireplace was burning nicely. Chris had always been good with making a fire. Nikki went over to check her husband out. He was thumbing through the music, looking for something else to put on.

"You know how niggas will start yelling, 'New DJ' if you don't keep it going," Chris said as he saw Nikki walking over.

"Okay, who isn't drunk?" Rick said, raising his glass up.

"I'm not," Jason said.

"Me either," Kay said.

"All right, this is the deal then, you *must* keep a full glass in your hand at all times. If I see anyone with an empty glass you have to take three shots. Deal?"

"Deal!" everyone yelled, heading to go fill up their

glasses. Lynda tripped on something, walking through the dining room and everyone started laughing.

"Fuck y'all," she said, laughing at her own clumsiness.

"You're gonna lose your license to drink if you keep that shit up," Kevin said.

"I'm fine," Lynda said, "trust me. I have a long way to go before I'm wasted."

"Well, let's get you there quicker," Kevin said, staring into Lynda's eyes.

As fine as Kevin was, Lynda couldn't take her eyes off Nikki. She was wearing some tight black pants with a shirt that had the back completely out. *Damn*, Lynda thought, *she's just beautiful.* She snapped out of her five-second daydream and held her glass up while Kevin filled it with more Merlot.

"Anyone else want wine?" Kevin asked.

"I do," Renee said. She was standing right behind him and when he spun around their lips damn near touched.

"My bad," Kevin said, gazing into her eyes.

Jason just happened to look across the room as Renee and Kevin were staring each other down. He didn't know why Kevin annoyed him so much when it came to Renee. To be honest, he was a little jealous of the brother. He was dark, in good shape, and funny, not that he himself thought he was a bad-looking guy, but he knew that Kevin was definitely a ladies' man. "The darker the berry, the sweeter the juice," he had overheard Renee say on the phone with Nikki one day. He always wondered who she was talking about that day and if she meant it.

"Hey, Jay, man, you better fill up that glass," Rick said.

"Right, man, I'm about to come your way," Jason said, barely smiling.

* * *

Renee walked over to the dining room table to grab some food, but it was all pretty much gone except for some crackers and fruit. Nikki was clearing it away and taking some stuff out of the freezer.

"Hey, Renee," she said, balancing a large tray on her right hand, "can you go have everyone get together in the living room? We're gonna start some games."

"Oh, shit, it figures," Renee said, "you and your *games.*" She spun around and started sending people toward the living room.

"All right," Nikki said, walking over to the group as they finished settling down on the couches and the floor. Pretty much wherever they could get comfy.

"We're going to play a raunchy version of the Newlywed game. All of the men sit on that side of the room and the women sit on this side with me." Everyone got up to take their respective places.

"I'm going to be asking the women questions and the men have to write down what you think your woman will say. Now if they—"

"Wait, wait," Kevin interrupted, "so I need to write the answer that I think Kay would say?"

"Exactly," Nikki said. "And, Kevin."

"Yeah?"

"Don't interrupt me again." She smiled. "Okay, now the twist is that every time you get an answer wrong, guys, your woman gets to walk over to one of the guys and whisper the nastiest thing she can think of in his ear."

"Where do you come up with this stuff?" Renee said.

"Yeah, I don't even think I know how to talk nasty," Rick said.

"Yeah, right, I'm sure you'll do just fine," Lynda said, rolling her eyes.

"Ready?" Nikki said.

"Yup," everyone said.

"Okay, this is just a little something to get the juices flowing. Take a piece of paper and a pen and pass the basket around," she said, handing a basket to Chris. After they got situated Nikki read the first question.

"How big do you think your woman thinks your dick is?" Nikki asked, giggling before she could get the entire question out.

"Um, do you have bigger sheets of paper?" Chris asked.

"Yeah," Jason said, "I need a bigger piece too."

"Just write your answers please, guys. Do you think she'll write four inches, six inches, or eight inches, et cetera?" Nikki said.

The guys were looking up in the air trying to come up with an answer. The women had already written theirs and were waiting patiently, trying to decide what they would whisper and whose ear they would whisper in.

"Time!" Nikki said. "You go first, Rick, since you're on the end."

Rick turned his paper over and held it up. He had written the words REALLY BIG.

"Listen, fellas, please play right," Nikki said, looking sad.

"All right, all right, all right," Rick said, turning his paper on the other side so everyone could see. He had written *eight inches*.

"Okay," Nikki said, "turn yours over, Lynda."

Lynda could barely keep from laughing. She had written *seven inches* on hers.

"All right, Lynda, you get to go whisper sweet nasty nothings into any man on the panel's ear."

Lynda was looking at the panel of men before her. She wished she could stand up and turn to her immediate right and walk in Nikki's direction, grab her, and tell her all the things she felt like doing at that moment.

"Hurry up," Nikki said, "who will you pick?"

Lynda walked over to Jason and stood in front of him. Then she stepped in between his legs as if she were about to give him a table dance. She leaned over, sticking her ass out in the air, and said things that made Jason's face turn bright red. Rick was leaning up out of his chair about to break his damn neck to hear what Lynda was saying. Jason was fidgeting in his chair. Lynda walked back toward the kitchen to fill her glass, then came and sat down. By the time she came back, Renee was leaned over Chris, and Chris had his hands on her lower back. Nikki was looking like she wished they were playing another game. Kay was last and she walked over to Chris also.

"Hey," Nikki said, "why did you both pick him?"

"We're twins," Renee and Kay said, both laughing hysterically. Kay leaned over and said her piece in Chris's ear.

"All right, can I just say that you men sucked at this first round?" Nikki said. "Now it's our turn. I'll give the next question, and if our answers don't match yours you get to pick one of the women and give her a passionate kiss on the neck."

"All right," Kevin said, sitting up straight in his chair.

Kay was looking at him like she wished her arm were five feet longer so she could slap his ass.

"Here's a question for us ladies," Nikki said, "so listen up, ladies. What is your man's favorite way to hit it?

A, from the back? B, missionary? C, from the side? D, going down on you?"

This time the women were struggling a bit and the guys were done quickly.

"Okay, now, when you say going down on you," Chris said, "where are we going?"

"Cute, Chris . . . real cute . . . you know what I'm talking about. Damn!" Nikki said.

"What? I'm just trying to pick the right answer."

"Time . . . time's up," Nikki said, smiling at Chris. "All right, you go first, Kay. What did you say Kevin's favorite position was?"

Kay turned over her paper and it read *from the back*.

"I didn't know you were such a freak," Renee said, looking at her sister.

"Me?" Kay said. "C'mon, that's not that freaky."

Kevin held up his answer and it matched Kay's.

"Okay, I'll go next," Lynda said, holding up hers. She had written *going down on you*.

Rick looked like his manhood had been stripped away. He held his up and it read *from the back*. It didn't match.

"Well, all right now," Rick said, standing up, adjusting himself and his pants. He searched the panel of women to see who he wanted. He walked over to Renee and put his lips on the left side of her neck. Her eyes closed and her smile turned to a real serious look immediately. She was getting turned on in front of everyone.

"Um, that's enough," Nikki said, tapping Rick on his back. He finally stopped and walked back over to the men's side.

Jason held his up next, and it said *from the back*. Renee had written *missionary*. Jason smiled at his chance to get her back for the kiss Rick had just given her that she enjoyed so damn much. He walked directly over to Nikki, put her face between his hands, and started to suck her neck as if it had honey on it.

"Ayy, man," Chris yelled, halfway joking, "don't be mad at me because Rick kissed your girl, damn."

Jason kept going and going until Nikki literally pulled out of his grip. Jason stared Renee down as he walked back to his chair.

"I think that's enough of that game," Kay said.

"Yeah," Kevin.

"Okay, let's just turn out all the lights and do whatever," Nikki said.

"Yeah, put on some good music and let's get loose," Kay said.

"Y'all ain't ready for that Marvin, are you?" Kevin asked, looking through the CDs.

"Before you put on more music," Rick said, "I need Nikki, Kay, and Chris to go take three shots since their glasses are sitting next to them empty." He had gotten them.

"Cheers," the ladies said, toasting the shots Rick poured, then downing them. Chris had already finished his.

"Hold up, I have one more game to make the dancing more interesting," Nikki said. "Everyone take a scarf out of this basket and tie it over your eyes before the lights go out. Remember what color scarf you have. Everyone should grab a partner to dance with once the lights are out and everyone is blindfolded. Just touch and feel until you feel a person you want to get down with. There are no rules here, just dance and really enjoy the music. When the song is done, exchange scarves with your partner. This is why it's important to

know what your own scarf looked like and that it's dark
as hell. When you get back to your side of the room
everyone will open their eyes and see who is holding
your scarf. Only you and your partner will know what
happened on the dance floor in the dark."

"Now, this one sounds like fun," Kevin and Jason
said, high-fivin' each other.

Everyone put their drinks down and grabbed a scarf
out of the basket. When the blindfolds were on, Nikki
tied her own scarf tight and hit Play on the CD player.
That famous whisper came through the speakers as
Marvin Gaye's voice vibrated throughout the hotel room.
"Let's Get It On" was an appropriate song for the night.

Nikki took a couple of steps toward the middle of the
floor, careful not to fall over anything, when she felt an
arm grab her. She couldn't tell who it was. She was pretty
sure it was Jason, though. He wore a real distinct cologne,
Issey Miyake, she thought. He was putting his hands all
over her and she didn't even object. She would just blame
her release of all inhibitions on the amount of liquor
they had all consumed. Chris popped up in Nikki's mind
for a brief moment as she wondered who he was dancing with and where his hands were. But her attention was
quickly diverted when she was firmly pulled toward her
partner and could feel that whoever it was had gotten
turned on pretty quick. The party had obviously escalated
to the next level. But there was yet another notch for it
to go.

Whoever Kevin was holding sure felt good, was all he
kept thinking to himself. The body felt all too familiar
and Kevin realized he had somehow found Kay in the
midst of all the groping and dancing that was going on.
He had no shame in putting his hands in all the places
he wanted them to go, and of course Kay let him. Why

not? His hands had visited those places so many times before. He put his tongue on her neck and heard a slight moan escape her. *Damn,* he thought to himself, *whoever I end up with tonight will not be disappointed.* He was ready to leave the party already.

Chris knew for sure that he was dancing with Renee. He could tell that the female was real tall and had a tiny waist. Had to be Renee. He was very conservative in how he danced with her. A little bit of grinding never hurt anybody, he thought, smiling to himself. He wanted to raise his scarf up just enough to be able to see what was going on in the rest of the room. It was very quiet and everyone had seemed to fall into this mood. The tone had been set, Chris realized. The party was just beginning.

Jason was enjoying himself too much with his partner. He couldn't help it, though. The most exciting part of it was that he couldn't determine exactly who it was. He had thought it was Nikki initially, but at one point during the song he put his hand on her back and it just didn't feel like it was her. Nevertheless, he was taking full advantage of the moment. He was ready to take whoever he was dancing with into one of the rooms and close the door behind them.

The song was finally ending and Nikki's voice filled the room.

"Take off your scarves and exchange it for your partner's scarf but keep your eyes closed until you're on your side of the room."

All the guys walked to one side of the room, taking off their scarves, while the ladies did the same. Everyone held their scarves up, and the expressions on people's faces were priceless. Nikki was the first one to recognize her scarf dangling in Jason's hand. He had a look of surprise on his face as if he hadn't expected it to be her either.

Chris realized he had been dancing with Kay the entire time. He had almost been right. He had thought it was Renee, but he was close enough. *Damn,* he thought, *her ass is tighter than it looks in those jeans she always wears.*

Kay had a guilty grin on her face, looking at Chris from across the room.

Kevin was doing all he could to keep his composure. He had been so close to Renee that he could smell her hair and hadn't even known it. The twin thing could be something else at times, he thought to himself. Renee was smiling at him from across the room, obviously a little drunk.

Meanwhile, Lynda realized she had been with her own husband the whole time. She knew it the minute he had grabbed her. She had enjoyed the dance, though, especially since she and Rick loved the song so much.

Lynda knew that the party was ending and that it would soon be time to go. She looked around the room, looking at each guy one by one, trying to imagine being with them all. She couldn't, though. Kevin was fine as hell, but she didn't think he liked her too tough. Jason was weird as hell and Chris was, well, he was Chris. He was like a brother to her. Her eyes moved across the room and landed on Nikki. She just watched her for what seemed like an eternity. She was watching her lips move as she talked to Kay and Renee. Just observing her body and how it had its own language in general. She had to admit that Nikki was more appealing to her than any of the men in the room. She needed a drink. A strong one.

Everyone was finishing up their drinks, all seemingly coming to the realization at the same time that the "real" party was about to begin. Chris walked up to Nikki and whispered in her ear, "I think they're actually nervous to wrap this part of the night up, because you know what that means."

"I know it," Nikki said. "Shit, I'm a little nervous myself." She walked over to the CD player and shut it off. That seemed to get everyone's attention and they looked up at her. "Time for the real party to begin," she said. "The ladies will be leaving in about five minutes. Ladies, your mystery man won't be too far behind you. We don't have to clean up, because I got a late checkout for tomorrow." It seemed as if Nikki was talking in slow motion, judging by the looks on everyone's faces.

"Hello?" Jason said, waving his hand in front of Kay's face.

"You ladies wake up and rise up outta here," Rick said, gesturing toward the front door.

"All right, already," Lynda said. "I have to go to the bathroom first. Try and get rid of some of this liquor in my system." Lynda left the living room and headed to the bathroom near the foyer up front. The voices in the living room began to sound more and more distant.

Lynda finished up in the bathroom and walked out into the foyer. She looked to her right and saw the bowl with all the keys sitting near the front door on a table. She walked toward the door to take a closer look into the bowl. She didn't know why, but she was drawn to it somehow. At that moment the bowl appeared to be full of lots of things, not just keys. Her marriage was in there; friendships were in that bowl, and even some fates that had yet to be determined. Her own fate included. Oh, and Nikki had put a ton of condoms in there. As close as they all were, they still planned to practice safe sex. She heard the ladies saying their goodbyes and headed back toward the living room. She hoped she didn't appear nervous. When she got back she realized that no one had even noticed she was gone, and she was glad.

All of the ladies had their coats on by the time Lynda got back. Kay handed Lynda her coat and her purse. Everyone was hugging and kissing their significant other. They were giving reassuring final words to the person that everything would end up just fine. Deep down inside, though, no one knew what would happen. They were all just hoping for the best, in a sense. The ladies walked through the hallway together and into the foyer where each of them also stopped to take a good look at the bowl filled with keys and condoms. They all grabbed one or two just in case.

"Bye," they yelled, shutting the door behind them. They didn't say much to each other outside standing by their cars. They all just got into their cars and pulled out of the hotel parking lot one behind the other.

Eight

Ecstasy

Kay was tired as hell when she got home after leaving the key party. She had drunk so much she couldn't believe she was still standing. She had a great time, though, and was anxious to see who was going to choose her key. If she had her choice she wanted it to be Chris. She would love to stick it to Nikki just for the sheer fun of it, not to mention she was a sucker for tall men and Chris was six-four and fine as hell. She couldn't help but think about who would pick her key. It all felt a little crazy, but she was looking forward to it.

D'Angelo was her choice of music for the night as she headed to her bedroom to get undressed.

"How does it feel?" Kay sang along while she searched through her lingerie drawer for something to wear. Kay just loved lingerie. She was the type of woman who would never be caught without a matching bra and panty set. She only wore silk nighties to bed, and when she and Kevin were getting their groove on, she would even go as far as leather. One time she broke out handcuffs and a whip, but quickly found out that Kevin wasn't into all that. A little sting on the booty was all she asked for, but Kevin could never do it without cracking up, which always spoiled the mood. He was such a clown sometimes; it got on her nerves. She wondered if he was only like that with her. She had noticed him looking at other women in the past and he had such a different vibe. He seemed a bit more serious, sexy even.

"Let's see, should I wear red? Black? This purple set is really nice. I think I'll wear this silk purple shorts set. I look cute in that. He's gonna think I'm crazy when he rolls up in here with me dressed like I'm his woman . . . but I figure I may as well play the part for tonight, right?" she said, talking to herself in the mirror.

Once Kay finished primping in the bedroom, she decided to grab a wine cooler, then lie on her gray and black love seat to wait for her mystery man. She had visions of wild, passionate, freak, nasty sex running through her mind as she drifted off into a deep sleep. Before she knew it she was knocked out. The bottle was still in her hand resting on her stomach. She didn't even hear her front door open.

He wasn't too familiar with Kay's place. He had been there only a few times when Kay and Kevin had the crew over for dinner once before. He called out to Kay, but got no answer, so he went down the short hallway toward the living room. There she was. He watched her, as she lay peacefully asleep on her back, her silk purple shirt rumpled just enough to expose the bottom of her breasts. She had an "inny," he noticed as he removed the drink from her hand and placed it on the floor. He smiled and sat down beside her.

"Kay," he called out to her again. She still didn't answer. He tapped her on the shoulder lightly "Kay . . . wake up," he said again. He was laughing at this point. He couldn't believe his luck. He couldn't believe she was sleeping as he sat there shaking his head, admiring her beauty. She really was gorgeous. Just one of those women that you couldn't argue whether or not she was fine. She just was. Her long silky black hair, that smooth brown skin. She even had cute feet. That purple accented it all nicely, he thought as he carefully brushed the hair out of her face. She smiled.

"Kay? You up?" he said again anxiously. He couldn't bring himself to wake her. He was a bit uncomfortable with this key party. He felt guilty about his past experiences with the escort. It just didn't seem fair that he got to participate in something like this as well. He had already stepped outside of their marriage, but Lynda had no idea. He just wished he could get Lynda to open up to him. All he wanted from her was a little sign that she was still in love with him. Lynda wouldn't budge, though.

He had to fight hard just to get a blow job sometimes. He was just frustrated. "Why does everything have to be about sex?" Lynda would ask him when they would get into it. She just didn't understand that it wasn't just the sex. It was the closeness. He couldn't tell how many times she'd pull away from him when all he wanted to do was hold her. "Sex is a very important part of a marriage, Lynda," Rick would say. "It's what separates friends from lovers, and I thought we were both." The night would always end with Lynda sleeping on the couch and Rick jacking off in the bedroom. He couldn't understand where things went wrong. When they were first married, it was like she couldn't get enough of him. Over the years it was like he just wasn't enough anymore. He had often thought she was having an affair, but he was never able to prove anything. Besides, what could he say if she was? "Now we're even"? He couldn't allow himself to go there. He loved her too much to think about her with another man. Kay started to squirm some more.

"Kay?" Rick said, hoping she was waking up. He wanted to shake her a bit and say, "Wake up, girl," but he just continued to stare at her. Then he glided his hand up and down the thigh that was hanging off the couch, inviting him to touch it. She had great legs. Her thighs were nice and thick, just the way he liked them.

"Mmmmmmm," she started to groan. Rick's face lit up. He took it as permission to explore a little more. His hands carefully creeped underneath her silk top across her breasts. Her nipples were hard, which got Rick riled up. Kay reacted a little differently than he expected. She started to twist and turn a bit and then her hands took over. She was touching herself, in ways that he'd only dreamed Lynda would. Kay was asleep but her hands were awake . . . wide awake. They had a mind of their own as they traveled up and down her entire body. Her purple shorts were invaded by her probing hands. Her groans started to heighten as her fingers started to thrust in and out of her wet pussy. Rick was feeling real good about now. His body was aching. He wanted her bad. It excited him just watching her. Lynda never masturbated in front of him. He caught her once and she got so pissed she didn't talk to him for a week. He was enjoying watching Kay get out of control and it excited him even more to know that it was his touch that initiated it.

The sight of Kay's body in ecstasy was enough to make him want to join in, so he did. He slid his hands up and down her smooth brown thighs, then in one quick motion pulled her shorts along with her underwear off and threw them on the floor. Kay continued to twist and squirm when Rick decided to taste her. His dick was rock-hard now. He was in control and loved it. His hands slithered across her body, up to her breasts, and started to squeeze them as he continued to plunge his tongue deep inside her. The added excitement finally woke Kay from her sleep. She was stunned when she witnessed what was happening, but that didn't stop Rick.

"Rick?" Kay said sweetly as she watched him have his way with her pussy.

Rick looked up when he realized she was awake. They gazed steadily in each other's eyes as he rose up and worked his way up her hot and trembling body. His body pressed against hers, and they started to kiss passionately. Kay could taste herself on his lips, but it didn't bother her. She was loving every bit of this moment. The excitement, the liquor, and D'Angelo were harmonizing as their bodies intertwined in ecstasy. Rick felt so good in her arms she couldn't help but wrap her legs around his hard body. She slid her hands under his sweater along his soft, creamy mocha skin.

"Mmmmmm," she continued to moan as Rick grabbed her ass and squeezed it. Rick then ripped her purple silk top off. The buttons went flying to the floor.

Kay laughed. "You planning on replacing that?" she said jokingly. Rick started to laugh too.

"This is so wild," Kay said.

"What?"

"Us . . . kissing . . . making out . . . I just never thought I would be able to do this so freely . . . I must be drunk" Kay said.

"Nah, you aren't drunk . . . just mesmerized by my charm."

"Whatever . . . I'm mesmerized by that tongue. What

are you thinking?" Kay asked, noticing Rick's changed mood.

"I'm thinking . . . thinking . . . I wanna tie you up."

"*What?*" Kay gasped.

"Yeah . . ." he said, pleased with his idea.

Rick got up and started looking around the living room. Kay sat up, watching Rick shuffle around looking for something to tie her up with. She was in awe of his nerve in thinking he could just come to her house and tie her up like she was some freak off the street. But at the same time she was intrigued with his boldness and arrogance. She was turned on by how crazy he was. Kevin would never have tied her up, let alone have her tie him up. She tried a couple of times and he just wasn't down. He was such a romantic, which worked for her for the most part. But sometimes she wanted to get a little buck wild, and this night with Rick was the perfect opportunity to do it. Rick remembered the scarf in his pocket from the party and pulled it out. He walked over to Kay smiling like he was the devil. Kay scooted to the back of the couch, naked, trembling with excitement and a bit of fear. After all, she didn't know what Rick was really capable of. She was fairly comfortable that he wouldn't hurt her. But she didn't know what his limits were.

"Rick?"

"Shhhhhh . . . don't . . . I won't hurt you . . . I promise . . . just relax."

Rick sat down beside her, gazing into her fearful eyes.

"You're so radiant, you know that?" he said, in awe of her beautiful, silky smooth complexion.

"Radiant? Wow, that's one I haven't heard before."

Kay's dark brown eyes pierced through his as she smiled.

Rick smiled too, as he kissed her eyes gently and then her forehead, each cheek, and then her lips. He wanted to assure her that he wasn't going to hurt her. Then he took his scarf and blindfolded her.

"What are you doing?"

"Just relax."

"I thought you were going to tie—"

"Shhhhh . . . I know . . . don't worry."

Kay's body was in flames. She was so wet she could feel the excitement flowing down her thighs, and then there was darkness. She could only smell Rick's cologne and feel his hands touching her everywhere.

"Mmmmmmmm . . . you're killing me," she whispered.

The passion was overwhelming. She started to breathe wildly as she let Rick explore her entire body with his hands and with his mouth. He touched her in places she never imagined she would be touched. Then he took her hands and ran them across his body. First his face. She could feel a slight stubble. He then took her fingers in his mouth and started to suck on them. She was getting more and more turned on. She wanted him desperately at this moment. She wanted to be the one in control. She was ready to fuck his brains out. Then she slid her hands across his chest and felt the curves of his body. Then, finally, she was holding his dick in her hands. It was a good size, smooth, hard, and throbbing.

Rick moaned as she stroked him up and down. He wanted her so bad and she wanted him. Rick removed the scarf from Kay's eyes and positioned her body until she was lying on her back on the couch. He tenderly stroked Kay's shoulders and then her forearms and hands. He took her arms and placed them above her head. He tied her wrists together tight.

Kay was shaking as she stared deeply into Rick's eyes. She thought her body would explode at that moment. Kay closed her eyes again and let Rick's hands travel all over her body. He turned her over and ran his hands all over her backside. Then his tongue began to do all the work as it slithered its way down to her spot.

"Mmmmmmm . . . you do it so good," Kay whispered, feeling completely out of control. She wanted to touch him but couldn't. She wanted to touch herself but couldn't. She felt tortured and loved it.

Rick couldn't get enough of Kay's pussy. He could eat it all night but decided he was ready for a little more. So he untied her, stood up, and swept her naked body in his arms and headed toward the bedroom. Kay felt like a princess being swept away by her prince. Rick was strong and lean. Kay's arms were clasped around his neck as she kissed him. He smelled so good, she thought. When they reached the bedroom, Kay became a bit nervous.

"No," she whispered.

"What's wrong?" Rick said, perturbed.

"Not here, not on the bed." Kay's conscience suddenly attacked her and she didn't feel comfortable having sex with Rick on the same bed that Kevin had made love to her so many times.

"Come on, Kay. Don't do this to me," Rick pleaded.

He was so fine, she thought. She couldn't believe that she never noticed that before. She let Lynda poison her mind against him over the years, telling her stories of how weak Rick was in bed and how he couldn't get her excited. She had never looked at him in a sexual way before tonight. She was astounded at how wrong Lynda was. His sexy, brown eyes met hers and she lost herself in them.

Rick put her down and decided to let her take the lead. He was a bit puzzled when she took his hand and led him toward the bed. He admired her from the back as her ass moved up and down sweetly. He wondered what changed her mind, but decided it was the wrong time to get into all that. Kay walked over and turned off the lights and lit a candle.

The dim light captured the silhouette of her body just right. Rick hadn't felt this way about Lynda in a long time, years even. Lynda never seduced him with candlelight or lingerie. She always wanted to get right down to business, almost as if she wanted to get it over with. Kay's patience enticed and excited him. Breathlessly, Kay began to undress Rick. She removed his sweater and pants slowly and provocatively as Rick watched. Her eyes drank in every ripple as she glided her sleek hands up and down his torso. *Damn,* she thought to herself as she finished undressing him. His naked body stood in front of her for the taking. There was no turning back now, they both thought. They came together hungrily and began to kiss, their tongues darting recklessly. Rick held her hot, trembling body tightly, feeling every curve. Kay stood on her tippytoes, pressing her breasts against Rick's hard chest.

"I want you so bad," Rick whispered, looking deeply into her eyes. A shiver ran through her as her body sank into the sheets. He took a deep breath and slid on top of her. Her sweet scent hypnotized him as he slid his tongue in her ear.

"Mmmmmmm," Kay moaned. She was ready. "Fuck me," she whispered.

Then he plunged inside her in one smooth stroke. Kay's eyes widened as she gasped in delight. This felt so right and she wanted to be nowhere else at that moment. They explored several different positions before they reached the one that would make them come. Kay lay facedown on the bed with Rick placed perfectly inside her throbbing pussy.

"You're gonna make me come," Kay said loudly as she gripped the sheets with her teeth.

"Yeah, Kay, come on," Rick said as he quickened his pace. Then she was up on all fours. He had her long hair in his hands, Kay's head was tilted back now, her eyes closed, and then she let out the loudest scream ever.

"Agghhhhhhh!"

Rick screamed in harmony with Kay as he pulled out, taking the condom off and releasing his passion all over her. His hand skated in ecstasy up and down her perfect ass.

"Ummmmmm," Kay continued to moan as she turned over and pulled Rick to her. She smiled at Rick; her dreamy eyes gazed into his. There was a strange peacefulness that came over them as they both lay in each other's arms and drifted off to sleep.

Nine

Man to Man

The roads were wet with rain and sleet by the time Chris left the key party.

Damn . . . I hope this sleet doesn't scratch up my Rover, Chris thought to himself as he turned up Stevie Wonder driving down Highway 75.

"There's a ribbon in the sky for our love . . . hmm-mmm," Chris sang, reminiscing about him and Nikki dancing on their wedding day. *How appropriate that I would hear our wedding song on the way to have sex with Lynda, or should I say inappropriate? I can't believe I let Nikki talk me into this,* he thought to himself as he exited the highway and slowly approached his home away from home, Rick and Lynda's crib.

Chris loved the wildness and impulsiveness of his wife; in fact, that was one of the things he loved most about her. But one of these days he wanted her to slow it down just a bit. He and Nikki had had conversations in the past where she hinted at exploring bringing other partners into the mix; they even went to a "swingers" party a while ago using an alias, but nothing ever happened. It was just for fun, just to quench Nikki's curiosity temporarily. In the past he always managed to talk her out of these crazy plans of hers. But this time, he decided to try a different approach. He felt that their marriage was tight and could sustain anything. He appreciated the fact that Nikki always respected his decisions and that she never let his "prude side," as Nikki called it, get in the way of their continued happiness. So, now he felt as if he were "in a crazy kind of way" returning the favor.

"What the hell?" he said to himself, pulling into the driveway. "My shit probably won't even get up, ha, ha." He laughed at himself, hoping he was wrong. It had been a long time since he'd been with another woman sexually. "I hope I don't go embarrassing myself. Yeah, right . . . what am I talking about. The ladies looooove 'Simon'"— Chris's little pet name for his dick.

The porch light was almost always on, but tonight there was only darkness to greet him.

Ding-dong . . .

Chris was getting a little nervous now. His palms began to sweat as if he were on a first date.

No answer.

"Hmmmm." He opened the glass storm door and knocked several times. Still no answer.

Is someone trying to tell me something? he thought as he went around to the side door. *Now, I know she's not trying to play games with my ass.*

Knock . . . knock . . . knock . . . Still no answer.

Chris was a bit baffled. *I know I gave her plenty of time to get here.* He proceeded to walk back to his car and wait. *I'm giving her ten more minutes and then I'm out!* he told himself.

The sleet had subsided a bit. The night was dark and

lonely as Chris lay back on his bucket seat, chilling. *I wonder what Nikki is doing right now*, he thought, still listening to his *Greatest Hits* CD. Stevie was his boy. He could always count on him when he was alone and in deep thought.

"Maaaan, I'm gonna hurt Lynda," he said, now sitting up. "She must have 'hoed' out and decided not to do it." Chris started up his Range Rover and decided to go home. He was secretly relieved that she didn't show up. He heard a car coming and looked up. It was her next door neighbor pulling into their garage. "Oh well, ten minutes are up! I'm outta here! I can't believe Nikki got me out in this nasty-ass weather involved in this crazy shit. She's going to loooove this. How convenient that my key partner didn't even show up. Knowing Nikki . . . her and Lynda probably planned it this way."

Hold up. He turned down Stevie and pulled over to the side of the road. He had to think for a second. *I can't go home. Nikki is there with her partner. Awwwww, this is fucked up. Now what should I do?* He figured he would head back to the Residence Inn, since Nikki gave him a key.

When Chris pulled up to the parking lot of the Residence Inn, their little spot had cleared out. He did recognize one car, though; it was Jason's burgundy Intrepid. "I wonder why Jay is still here," he said to himself. He stepped out of the car, racing to the door to get out of the rain.

Jason was lit up when Chris approached him. "Jay? You all right, man?" Chris said, walking into the suite. Jason looked up at Chris and smiled.

"Chrrrrrrrris . . . what up?" he said, slurring.

"What's going on? What are you still doing here?" Chris asked, concerned. Looking around the room, he saw empty bottles that had been half-full when they had all left.

"Well, it looks like I'm the last man out," Jason said as he scooted over on the sofa, allowing Chris to sit down.

"After you and Rick left I chatted with Kev for a second and then we decided to head out. He left before me, though. I went and got my coat and went to reach for a key on the way out. To my surprise . . . no key! I was like, 'What the hell? Where are the keys?' But by then I realized that I was the only one left in this muthafucka . . . Kevin left, you left, Rick was gone . . . and my baby was gone."

"There was supposed to be a key for all of us, right?"

"Ahhhhh, I don't give a shit anyway . . . I really didn't want to do this in the first place," Jason said, throwing his hands up in disgust. "Your babe is whacked!"

"Hold up . . . hold up . . . don't go calling my babe out 'cause you didn't get a key . . . you know you were down for this shit from the start . . . I didn't hear you complaining when Nikki was explaining the rules . . . and I sure as hell didn't hear you complaining the other night when we were playing spades." Chris was getting a little pissed. He got up and faced Jason. "Look, man . . . what's really going on? You've been acting a little strange lately. Is something going on with you and Renee?"

Chris realized that Jason was drunk, so he toned his anger down a notch. He figured he'd give him the benefit of the doubt. Chris was always the peacemaker in the group. He wasn't above kicking someone's ass, but it had to be the last resort. He didn't consider himself to be a violent man. He felt he could always talk his way out of anything. So he sat back down, and put his hand on Jason's shoulder.

"Jay, man . . . why did you agree to do this? You obviously have a problem with it . . . that's obviously why you got yourself all plastered."

"I wanted to please her . . . do you believe that?" Jason said. "I wanted to make her happy . . . how crazy is that? How crazy is it when you agree to let another man fuck your woman just to make her happy?" he said, laughing. "I mean, Renee and her girls are so tight. She would never have forgiven me if I told her she couldn't be a part of this. She would have told me I was being lame . . . that I wasn't open-minded enough."

"What!" Chris said with a surprised tone. "Who the hell are you talking about? Is this the same Renee I know?" Chris was looking at Jason as if he were someone else. "Look, Jay, I don't know what's going on . . . but you better go get your girl."

"What do you mean?" Jason said, looking puzzled. "What do you mean go get her? Do you think I wanna walk up in her place and into that scene? No, thank you!"

"No, that's why I'm telling you to go get her now before it's too late."

"It's already too late . . . even if I do catch her in time . . . she won't forgive me for this. She'll be all confused and embarrassed and shit. I don't even want to deal with the look on her face if I roll up in there tripping."

"Oh, it's like that between you two now?"

"Well . . . things have been a little shaky lately . . . let's just say, I'm probably the last person she's thinking about right now."

"Come on, Jay . . . girls love that shit . . . charging through the door, gallantly . . . sweeping them off their feet . . . rescuing them from the biggest mistake of their life," Chris said, elbowing Jason.

"Whatever, maaan . . . only you and Nikki believe in that Romeo and Juliet shit. In the real world . . . women need to feel like they're in control. They like to be the one that makes the decisions. All they want to do is take advantage of some poor desperate fool like me who's lonely and confused, so they can control them and then fuck their head all up."

Chris stopped smiling and looked at Jason—concerned again.

"Jay, are you all right? Is this Renee you're talking about? Renee is one of the sweetest, most sophisticated women I've met. She loves you, man. She chose you out of all the other men out there . . . she chose your ass . . . she agreed to marry you. Do you know what that means? Sure, she's feisty like all sistas, but that's what we love about our black women, right?" Chris said, thinking about Nikki.

Jason stood up and grabbed one of his Marlboro Lights. He lit his cigarette and inhaled it as if it were his last breath. He knew that Chris didn't understand where he was coming from. He didn't understand it himself. This deep resentment he had for women. He still loved his mother and didn't understand how he could. He tried to convince himself that she was sick when she would come at him. She didn't know what she was doing. But what he couldn't answer was why he let her do it. What did that mean? What kind of freak would have sex with his own mother? He couldn't get past it. He couldn't. Chris was looking at him. He decided to chill out. He didn't want Chris thinking he was nuts.

"So, Chris . . . how is it that you're okay with this shit? I mean, your babe was the one who put this all together. Don't you wonder why? Don't you ever think it's because she's not satisfied?"

"Nope," Chris said confidently.

"Look, I know this shit is off the chain. I know that there aren't a whole lot of couples that would even consider something like this, let alone do it. But we're different, Nikki and I. I know she loves me. It's not that she's not satisfied with me . . . she's not satisfied with life and the rules that come with it. I can't get her to see that we all have to follow the same rules. She doesn't want to hear that. She doesn't want to follow rules that forbid her to feel passion. She doesn't see the harm in something like this as long as we both agree. She sees it as eight friends sharing something deep and erotic. Something that no one else would ever think of doing because they're afraid . . . afraid of living life to its fullest. I understand that part of her . . . her need to fulfill this fantasy . . . and I'm convinced that my support turns her on . . . as much as she's probably turned on right now with her key partner, if not more."

The silence in the room was deafening. Jason stood in awe of Chris as he went on and on about Nikki's sex game. He finally saw the magic Nikki and Chris shared . . . he understood why they still kissed each other at the nightclub even though there were a thousand other women in the room . . . why they played "footsies" underneath the table when they thought no one else noticed . . . why Nikki looked at Chris the way he wished Renee would look at him. He finally understood what real love looked like . . . and it made him sad. He didn't have that with Renee. He never had it with any woman, and he never would.

"Jay? Hey . . . Jason?"

"Wha . . . what? Oh, sorry, Chris . . . I guess I kinda zoned out for a second."

"I didn't mean to get all deep on you, but I just

wanted you to know that it's okay if you don't want Renee to do this shit. I'm not saying it's not crazy . . . this is about as crazy as it gets. But I trust my wife and that's all there is to it. You have to remember," Chris continued, "Nikki and I have ten-plus years under our belt. That's a long time to love someone. You and Renee are just starting out. You don't need this kind of drama this soon in your relationship. What's it been . . . six months? Has it even been a year? Yeah . . . I can see why this is making you crazy. Frankly I was a bit surprised when Nikki told me you guys agreed to this. Go get her, man . . . if that's what you wanna do. She'll be all right."

Jason got up and lit another cigarette. "You're right, man. I'm out. I'm going to tell her to squash this and come home with me instead. Who do you think picked her?"

"I don't know . . . probably Rick."

"Why do you think it's Rick?" Jason said as he started to get upset again at the thought of Renee with someone else.

"I don't know . . . I was just throwing shit out there . . . it could be either one of them," Chris said, trying to keep Jason as calm as possible.

"Oh, you purposely didn't say Kevin 'cause you think she's got a thing for him, right?"

"What?" Chris said, now knowing it was time to change the subject. "Naw, man, like I said, I was just throwing shit out there. Come on, let's get out of here." Chris got up and put his arm around Jason and started to walk him to his car.

"You straight to drive?" Chris said.

"Yeah, I'm cool, man . . . I'm cool . . . I just hope I'm not too late. Damn, it's cold out here," Jason said, shivering.

"I know, this rain is a bitch!" Chris said, pulling his coat over his head while running to his car. "Hey, Jay . . . good luck, man . . . and look . . . don't trip if you're too late. Remember, you told her she could do it and she thinks you're doing it . . . so go easy on her when you see her, or should I say go easy on him? regardless of what's up. She'll be straight," he promised as he eased his way into his truck.

Yeah, right, Jason thought to himself. *If it's too late to stop her things may get ugly.* He sped out of the parking lot of the Residence Inn and headed toward Renee's place.

Ten

Awakening

Nikki ran through her front door straight to the kitchen once she left the Residence Inn. She grabbed a Red Dog out of the fridge, jumped up on her kitchen counter, and kicked off her black leather boots. She started chugging the beer down as if it were Kool-Aid as she reflected on the key party. She was pretty confident everyone had a good time, and that made her feel good. She wondered how things would be tomorrow. She hoped her friends could handle the night ahead of them. She thought about what a great marriage she and Chris had. She was able to act out one of her fantasies while still including the love of her life and all of her friends. What could be better than that! She loved Chris more than words could say. He always allowed her to explore her sexuality freely, and she never did things he didn't agree with. As she reached in the fridge for her second beer, she heard someone walking around in her living room. She was nervous and excited at the same time.

"Hello? Is anyone there?" she said.

She tiptoed around the corner and asked who was there again, but no one answered.

When she entered the living room she was a bit startled and then confused. Lynda was sitting on her big tan and black sofa with her long legs crossed, swaying back and forth. She had a strange smile on her face as Nikki approached her.

"Lynda? What's up? What are you doing here? Why aren't you at home?"

Lynda didn't say a word, she just started shuffling around in her black Coach duffel. Nikki walked over and sat down beside her. She was perturbed.

"What are you looking for?" Nikki questioned.

"Shhhhhhhh, hold on a minute . . . I know it's here somewhere . . . ahhhhh, here it is."

Lynda pulled out a key . . . Nikki's house key. She held the key in the air to show Nikki.

"Lynda . . . you're tripping . . . what are you doing with that?"

Nikki was puzzled. She knew that Lynda always had a secret crush on her, but this was a bit extreme. They never really talked about what had happened in college unless they were drinking. No one knew about it, not Kay, Renee, or their husbands for that matter. Sometimes Nikki would notice Lynda's dreamy brown eyes roaming whenever a diva type at a club or restaurant would walk by. She would just look at Lynda and smile whenever she caught her.

Lynda scooted over to Nikki on the couch. She got so close she could smell the beer on Nikki's breath.

"Do you have any more beer?" Lynda asked as if nothing out of the ordinary was going on.

"Yeah, I'll get it."

"No." Lynda hopped up, took off her beige wool coat, and headed toward the kitchen. "I'll get it."

"Lynda, what's going on? Why are you here?" Nikki yelled from the living room.

"Why am I here? Hmmmmm, why am I here?" Lynda said to herself, confused. She didn't have an immediate answer for Nikki. She made it to the kitchen doorway, turning up the beer she had just gotten out of the refrigerator. Lynda took a deep breath, looking confused as ever herself.

Nikki couldn't help but notice how put together Lynda looked. She was wearing an electric-blue fitted turtleneck tucked into a black A-line miniskirt, black tights, with knee-high, black leather boots. Lynda had such great style, Nikki thought.

"Why do you ask?" Lynda finally said, knowing exactly why Nikki asked.

"I ask because I know you as well as I know myself. I know that you wouldn't have come over here with my key if you didn't have something up your sleeve."

"Like what?" Lynda asked as she walked back to the couch unzipping one boot and then the other.

Nikki just looked at Lynda with that "you know what I'm talking about" look on her face.

"I'm here to be with you."

"Be with me?"

"Yes, you know better than anyone that I've always had a thing for women. You just happen to be the woman who opened my eyes to my true feelings, Nikki. I guess I never told you how much our experiences in college affected me. After our freshman year I never called you, remember?"

"We just sort of got out of touch, right?" Nikki asked.

"No, Nikki. I knew then that I had stronger feelings for you than I was willing to admit to you, or even to myself for that matter. I just thought that the old adage out of sight, out of mind was the cure. You know, a quick fix. I just tried to forget about you. But I realized I couldn't. I loved you. And I still do. I want you one last time, Nikki, because I know we'll never be together in the end."

Nikki didn't say a word. For once, she was speechless. She could feel herself blushing. She wanted to run as far away as possible, yet she couldn't find the strength to move. Her body lay limp. She hadn't expected Lynda to be in her living room, for one thing. And second, she damn sure hadn't bargained for Lynda to come over and lay it all out like she had. It excited her to know that Lynda wanted her in that way. She could feel her body slowly becoming inflamed. Nikki knew that she herself was far from being a lesbian, but she had thoughts of other women that made her know that she was a lot freer with her sexuality than most heterosexual women. It didn't disgust her to see two women together intimately at all. She was comfortable with that. Even her closest friends knew that much about her. They might not have completely understood it, but they accepted it for what it was. Kay and Renee thought she and Lynda were both weird when it came to that kind of stuff. They would always tease Nikki and Lynda about what freaks they were, but Nikki never cared.

"Nikki, are you okay? Nikki . . . Nikki . . . helloooooo, are you there?" Lynda was a bit flushed herself. She didn't mean to blurt it out quite like that. She snapped her fingers to get Nikki's attention.

"Huh . . . what did you say?"

"I'm sorry, girl. I didn't mean to scare you," Lynda

said as she took Nikki's hand and intertwined her fingers with hers.

"I know what you're thinking, and to answer your question, Rick and I are as good as we can be under the circumstances. This has nothing to do with him and everything to do with me. We have been going to counseling and it seems to be helping, but there is still a void in my life . . . something Rick can't fill."

"Really?" Nikki asked, gazing into Lynda's eyes.

"Yes, really . . . and I need to know if that void is you. I need to know if you are the reason that I can't make love to my husband without seeing your face and imagining that I'm touching your body. I have to know why you make me want to be with a woman when it's the last thing on this earth I should ever imagine really doing. I mean, I'm a married woman, Nikki. But I know that I'm in love with you."

Lynda's eyes started to well up with tears.

"Don't . . ." Nikki said, gently wiping away the tear that had started to fall from Lynda's eye. "Don't say another word," and then Nikki kissed Lynda. The first kiss was just a friendly one. But then something clicked and they started to recreate the scene from years ago. Lynda's soft lips parted, welcoming Nikki's warm and inviting tongue. They were in too deep to even think about stopping this time.

"Mmmmm," Lynda started to moan as she cradled Nikki's face in her warm hands.

Lynda's lips were smooth and full. Nikki always loved Lynda's lips. Lynda always thought they were too big . . . but Nikki thought they were just right. She used to tease Lynda about them. "I bet you suck a mean dick with those lips," she would say. "That's right!" Lynda would reply.

Lynda started to get heated. She could feel her pussy getting wetter and wetter. She took Nikki's hand and placed it under her skirt so she could feel her excitement. Nikki didn't stop her. To Lynda's surprise, Nikki moved her panties to the side and felt it. Then she put her finger in it. "Damn, you're so wet," Nikki whispered, "you're making me crazy." Nikki wasn't thinking. She was in another world, one she had never intended on being in again. She took her hands out of Lynda's panties and the smell of their passion took away all their inhibitions. Lynda teased Nikki's nipples with her tongue, marveling at the way the firm, velvety sensation inside her mouth ignited passion beyond her best lovemaking with Rick. They were caught up in the moment . . . a moment of awakening. Lynda then looked at Nikki intensely. She took her hands and stroked Nikki's face and moved them up throughout her wavy, silky hair. Her hands were soft and gentle, Nikki thought to herself as she closed her eyes and rolled her head back in ecstasy.

Lynda loved it. She wanted time to stand still. She had been wanting this for a long time. As she stared into Nikki's eyes, she got up slowly and started to undress. First her turtleneck, then her skirt, then her tights. A matching blue bra and panty set remained. Nikki knew it would be a thong. That was all Lynda wore. Lynda had one of those asses every black man dreamed about. It was attached to her perfectly flat stomach, twenty-four-inch waist, and 34-B breasts. She took good care of herself. "None of that fast food shit for me," she would always tell her girls when they were kicking it. She ran four miles every morning and lifted weights five days a week. Nikki was always jealous of Lynda's body, even though she had a great body of her own. Nikki's body just wasn't the traditional "black girl" body. Nikki had 36-C breasts and no ass. The best part of her body was her legs . . . so she was always told.

Nikki watched as Lynda undressed.

"Nice panties," Nikki told Lynda, smiling. She felt so at ease with Lynda. She was surprised at how comfortable she felt with her sexually. The experience of another woman's body could not compare to the sense of completion she had whenever she was with Chris. But it was a deeply sensual connection, a new exploration of the depths of her desires that heightened her sense of uninhibitedness. It was perfect that she could share this special moment with her best friend.

Lynda didn't wait for Nikki to take off her clothes. She walked over to Nikki, who had also stood up, and kissed her passionately. She loved kissing her. Her lips were soft and wet. She started to kiss her neck and then let her tongue travel across her throat to her breasts. Lynda slid Nikki's shirt off her shoulders and let it fall to the floor. Gazing into her eyes, she unclasped Nikki's black lace bra and slid her black silk panties off. She laid Nikki's naked body on the couch, then leaned over her, caressing her body. They were both shivering with desire . . . bound together in a maze of passion . . . their hips moving and grinding in sync with one another. Lynda had always been intrigued with giving another woman pleasure. She wanted to be in control. She continued to kiss Nikki's breasts. Then her tongue circled around her nipples.

"Mmmmmm," Nikki moaned in sheer delight. She was on fire. She hadn't prepared herself for what Lynda did next. She couldn't believe what was happening. She was so turned on. Chris had "gone down" on her a million times, but not quite like this. Lynda knew exactly where to go and where to put her tongue. Her skillful touch produced such passion for Nikki. It was beyond anything she could have dreamed. Her eyes were open as she watched Lynda. Her body was so hot she thought she would faint. And then it happened, "Ooooooooo oooohhhh . . . Yeah . . . Don't stop . . . I'm gonna come," Nikki said with a quivering tone. "Ahhhhhhhhhh . . ."

She was so loud Lynda started to laugh. "Damn, girl . . . does Chris make you scream like that?"

Nikki started to laugh too . . . as they both lay side by side, dripping with sweat, feeling nothing but pleasure.

"Whew . . . damn, girl. Who have you been practicing on?" Nikki joked, breathing heavily.

"Nikki . . ." Lynda whispered. "Thank you . . ." And she started to tear a little.

"Shhhhhhh," Nikki said, hugging Lynda tightly. "You don't have to thank me. Just make yourself happy, Lynda. I think you have some answers now. You can't keep living a lie. If you didn't gain anything else from tonight, at least now you know what you have to do. You know what you have to do," Nikki told Lynda quietly.

Eleven

Fortune

Renee was pacing up and down her two-story condominium as restless as ever. She couldn't keep still with all the nervous energy she had bubbling inside her. She'd had a blast at the key party, but now she felt scared as hell. This just wasn't her speed. She had always been classified as the "quiet twin." She was the voice of reason, the smart one, always in control of her life. Kay had always been there to balance her out. To make her life interesting in many ways. She was grateful for their talk the other day. It made her feel more confident of her decision to go through with the party. She was so concerned about Jason and what he would think if she even considered participating in this. She was surprised when he agreed to it so easily, but she knew he only agreed to it to please her. That actually scared her a little. But she decided to put all of that behind her tonight. She and Jason had had a good time at the party. She left him on good terms and she was ready to accept her fate tonight.

Hmmmmmm, what should I wear? Should I change? she thought, admiring herself in the maple-wood full-length mirror in her bedroom. She was wearing cherry-red slacks with a silk red tank top. She had wanted to stand out at the party. Renee always dressed sexy yet subtle. She actually wanted to be enticing for once. To show the guys what she had to offer under those jeans and T-shirts she always wore. "The Lady in Red" as Kevin had referred to her all night. She had thoughts of Kevin in her head as she started twirling herself around, day-dreaming. *He looked so handsome tonight*, she thought. *He was wearing the hell out of that cream, ribbed turtleneck sweater. Mmmmm and those black pants . . . well, let's just say . . . have mercy . . . what an ass! Hold up! What am I doing?* Renee said, opening her eyes, snapping back to reality. *I'm tripping, I need to stop thinking about that man. Kay's man, to be exact.*

Renee decided against changing her clothes and went into her bathroom to brush her teeth. She reached for a scrunchy to pull her hair out of her face. *Damn, I'm feeling a little tipsy. Those White Russians were no joke.* Just then, she heard someone walking around downstairs. "Oh, shit . . . I think he's here," she said, hurriedly rinsing her mouth and wiping her face with a towel. She started down the stairs that led to her living room, but saw no one. "Is someone there?" she said, now peeking around the corner, heading toward the kitchen. *Hmmm . . . I thought I heard someone. This is actually kinda creepy now that I think about it,* she thought to herself. When she made it back to the living room she was startled. There he stood on her oriental rug. A tall, chiseled piece of chocolate. His hands were in his pockets when he flashed her that beautiful smile of his. All she could do was blush.

"Hi, Kevin," she said, cheesing.

"Hey, Renee," he said, walking toward her.

"So, did you plan this or what?" Renee said, shoving Kevin.

"Come on, Renee . . . you know your key was the last one I wanted to pull," Kevin said, still smiling. He was feeling a bit nervous himself. He was serious, though. The last key he had wanted to pull was Renee's. He could have handled this with anyone else but her. He didn't trust himself when he was with her. There had been so many times in the past when he wanted to sweep her in his arms and make mad, passionate love to her. And tonight he was getting permission to do just that, and it scared him. Terrified him was more like it.

"I was just kidding, Kevin . . . I know you didn't want to pull my key," Renee said, looking up at his sexy brown eyes. "This whole thing is crazy anyway." She plopped down on her plush, navy blue love seat.

"Awww, girl, don't even try it . . . you know you're an undercover freak," Kevin said, sitting down beside her.

"Ha, ha . . . very funny. So what do we do now?" Renee asked Kevin, turning her body to face his.

"What do you mean? We fuck, that's what! Ha, ha, I'm kidding . . . I'm kidding," Kevin said, cracking up.

"Kevin, will you be serious for a minute?" Renee said, taking his hand.

Her hands were baby soft, Kevin thought to himself. It amazed him sometimes that Kay and Renee were identical twins. He never had a problem telling them apart. Renee was so different from Kay. He had known that the first day he laid eyes on her. Everything about her was different. Her touch, her smell, her smile . . . he could go on and on. He had studied her over this past year. Every curve, every inch.

"Kevin!" Renee snapped.

"Huh? Oh, I'm sorry, Renee," Kevin said, returning to earth.

"What I'm trying to say is that we obviously don't have to do this tonight," Renee said. "Can you imagine what Kay would say if she knew you picked my key? I mean, we just had a long talk and she said she was cool with what happened way back in the day with all that spin-the-bottle crap, but I really don't know if she meant it."

"That's cool, Renee," Kevin said, secretly disappointed. "Not that Kay's going to believe that we didn't do anything anyway."

Renee let go of Kevin's hand. She didn't know what he meant by that. Did he want to go ahead and do it? Her heart was beating a million miles per second. She wanted him so much at that moment. She wanted nothing more than to grab his beautiful face and kiss the shit out of him. She hadn't forgotten what a good kisser he was.

"Hey, let's play some music." Renee jumped up, breaking the silence.

"Cool," Kevin said, relieved, since he was just milliseconds away from kissing her.

"Prince?" Renee said.

"Yeah, that'll work," Kevin said, getting up to join her over by the stereo system.

"I have his greatest hits. It's the bomb! It's got all his old-school jams on it."

"Does it have 'Adore'? That's my favorite."

"Yep, and 'Do Me Baby' too."

"Controversy" was the first song to play. She and Kevin started dancing. They were doing all the old-school dances, having a ball, reminiscing of their college days and what fools they used to be when they were younger. They laughed and danced through the first couple of songs and then Kevin's jam came on. He decided to do his best impersonation of Prince.

"Here we are in this big ole empty room," Kevin started singing to Renee.

". . . staring each other down," Renee chimed in.

". . . you want me just as much as I want you . . . let's stop fooling around," they both continued to sing.

"May I have this dance?" Kevin said to Renee, extending his hand.

"Why, certainly," Renee said, curtseying. She took his hand and they walked toward each other. They stopped and looked in each other's eyes for a moment. The room was still. They weren't singing anymore. His eyes pierced through hers. Kevin lifted his hand to her face and stroked her cheek.

"Damn, you're beautiful," he whispered.

Renee took his hand and removed it from her face and placed it around her waist. She moved in closer to him and laid her head on his chest. She could feel his heart beating rapidly as she closed her eyes and lost herself in his arms. He laid his cheek on her head, holding her tightly. Their bodies rocked to the music. His hand slid carefully underneath her shirt. He could feel her silky skin as his hand glided all over her back. She didn't stop him; instead, she moved closer, so close she could feel how turned on he had gotten.

"Kevin?"

"Yes?"

"I . . . I . . ."

Then the music stopped.

"What is it?"

"Nothing," she said, breaking from his arms. "Damn,

we were jamming, weren't we?" she said, trying to break the mood.

"Yeah . . . we were," Kevin said, going along with her.

"I'm hungry, do you want something to eat?"

"What you got?" Kevin said with a devilish grin, looking her up and down.

"I meant *food*, Kevin . . . *food*," she said, heading toward the kitchen. "Let's see . . . I have leftover KFC . . . two-day-old Chinese food . . . salad . . . Jell-O . . . whipped cream . . . and, ooooh, chocolate cake," Renee said, licking her lips.

"Break it all out," Kevin said, admiring Renee from the back.

"You pig."

"What? I mean, you know . . . I just wanna have some options," Kevin said, bumping her out of the way so he could get at the food.

"I know," Renee said. "We can have a carpet picnic."

"A carpet picnic," Kevin said, mocking Renee.

"Yeah . . . it will be fun. I'll go grab a blanket . . . you get all the food out . . . oh, grab some of that wine too," Renee said, halfway up the stairs toward her bedroom.

Kevin pulled out all the food as he was told and grabbed a bottle of Pinot Grigio out of the wine rack. He had been at Renee's enough times to know where to find the wineglasses, so he took it upon himself to pull two out of the cabinet to the right of the sink. When he made it back to the living room, Renee was already there sitting Indian style on a fluffy yellow blanket. Kevin couldn't help but stare. She was so fine, he thought.

"Lady in Red," Kevin said, smiling at Renee.

Renee just looked up at him and blushed. She loved it when he called her that. She knew red was his favorite color. He had called her that before. Subconsciously, she thought she might have worn red tonight just for him.

"Damn . . . have you done this before?" Kevin said, referring to the whole picnic setup.

"Yeah." She chuckled. "Jason and I do it from time to time."

Kevin's smile dropped. That was the first time Jason's name was mentioned since he had been there. It kinda brought him back to reality. It was actually a good thing. Renee noticed a slight change in Kevin's mood when he walked over to sit down.

"Did you get it all?" she said, referring to the food he had tucked everywhere.

"Yeah . . . I just need to get the wine," he said.

"I'll get it," she said, jumping up and running to the kitchen.

As she ran past, a scent of Ralph Lauren perfume lingered there with Kevin. He loved that scent and she always wore it, teasing him unknowingly. While she was in the kitchen he laid out all of the food on the blanket. The same blanket she and Jason had shared so many times before. He wanted to burn it or cut it up into tiny pieces. *What the hell is wrong with me?* Kevin said to himself. He needed to get it together. Jason was his friend and Renee was his girlfriend's sister . . . he was out of control. He wanted to run as far away from Renee as possible at this moment. He knew he always had strong feelings for her, but he never imagined they would be this strong. He could always control his desire for her in the past because Kay or Jason would usually be around. He'd never spent one-on-one time with her before, not like this. He wasn't sure he could hold back his feelings much longer.

"I'll put some more music on," Kevin said.

"Oh, okay. I'm still working on getting this wine bottle open." She could hear Sade playing now.

"Damn, this wine opener is cheap," she said to herself, still struggling to get it open. Then she felt Kevin's warm body pressed up against her back.

"You need some help with that?" he whispered in her ear.

"Kevin . . . you scared me," she said. Her body was instantly set on fire. Both arms reached around her as he took the wine bottle in his hands.

"Let go . . . I'll take it from here," he said. She removed her hands from the wine bottle and just stood there burning in his arms.

Pop!

"There you go," Kevin said, pleased with himself.

"Cool . . . now let's eat," Renee said, running from his arms toward the living room. Renee wasn't only running from his arms . . . she was running from her feelings. She didn't want to feel the things she was feeling tonight. She and Jason had just gotten things straightened out. She didn't want to mess things up between them. She told herself that this was just a game, but from the time she saw Kevin standing in her living room she knew it was much more than that. She loved Jason, but there had always been something between her and Kevin that she could not explain. He made her laugh. She loved that about him. Not to mention how fine he was. Damn!

"Sade? Are you trying to depress me or something?" Renee said, grabbing a piece of chicken.

"What? Sade's deep as hell and sexy as all get out. Don't hate on a sista now."

"Hate? Come on, Kevin . . . don't get me wrong . . .

Sade is my girl and all that, but I usually only play her when I feel like crying."

"Awwww, you women kill me with that. Why would you play something for the sole purpose of crying? I mean, that's sadistic."

"Well, I don't play her for the sole purpose of crying . . . but when I'm in a somber mood and feel like crying . . . she's the one I want to listen to," Renee said, taking a sip of wine.

"Well, don't go crying on me now," Kevin said, throwing a fortune cookie at Renee. "Here, open that. Let's see what your fortune is."

Kevin broke his cookie open. "Life is like a box of chocolates. Awww, that's lame . . . that's not a fortune. Isn't that a line from that movie with Tom Hanks?" he asked.

"Yeah, *Forrest Gump*."

"Yeah . . . that's it . . . *Forrest Gump* . . . fortune cookies just aren't what they used to be. Well? What does yours say?"

Renee looked up at Kevin. She didn't want to read her fortune.

"Well?" Kevin said, still waiting.

"Ummmmm . . . it's just as pitiful as yours," Renee said, trying to dodge the question.

"Let me see it," Kevin said, grabbing it from Renee's hand.

"*Kevin!*" Renee screamed. "*Give it back!*"

Kevin got up and started running. Renee jumped up and ran after him.

"Kevin! Stop playing."

"What's the big deal?" Kevin said, running through the hallway toward the dining room. Renee caught up with him and jumped on him, tackling him to the floor.

"Give it here," she said, trying to grab it from his hands. She was straddling him on the dining room floor, desperate to get that fortune back. Kevin had his hands above his head so she couldn't reach it.

"You're tripping, Renee . . . what does it say?"

"I told you it's stupid. Just give it to me."

"Say the magic word," Kevin teased.

"Pleeeeeeeease," Renee pleaded.

"Okay . . . okay," Kevin said, sitting up and giving Renee the fortune. Neither of them had realized how close they were until now.

"Am I heavy?" Renee asked.

"Yeah, right," Kevin said. "All 105 pounds of you."

"Whatever, Kevin . . . I weigh more than that," Renee said, trying to get up.

"What's wrong . . . you stuck?" Kevin said with that devilish grin again.

"Ahhh, just a little bit . . . could you let me go please?" Renee said, wishing she could sit in his lap forever. The tension was thick in that dark dining room.

"Your wish is my command," Kevin said, lifting himself along with Renee off the floor. Now they were standing, facing one another.

"So, let me ask you something," Kevin said, gazing into her eyes.

"What?" Renee said, drinking every word that came out of his mouth.

"What were you going to say to me earlier when we were dancing?" Kevin said, backing her up against the dining room wall.

"Was I going to say something?" Renee asked.

"Yeah . . . you were in my arms and we were dancing and you started to say 'I' and then you didn't finish."

"Oh . . . that. You know what, Kevin. I don't even remember what I was going to say . . . let's just forget it, okay?" she asked, hoping Kevin would drop it.

"Cool," Kevin said, disappointed. "No pressure. You still hungry?"

"I could eat some of that chocolate cake," Renee said, looking Kevin up and down.

"Come and get it," Kevin said, smiling.

"You're funny," Renee said.

"Ohhhhh, that cake . . . my bad," Kevin said, laughing. "All right, girl . . . let me leave you alone." He backed away from Renee.

"I appreciate it," Renee said, relieved.

They headed back to the living room and continued to eat.

"This cake is the bomb," Renee said, shoving a huge piece in her mouth.

"Damn, girl . . . I didn't know you could eat like that," Kevin said, impressed. He loved a woman who could eat. Kay was such a health nut she never let her hair down to really enjoy her food. She was always counting calories and getting on Kevin about something unhealthy he was eating. He appreciated it, but it still drove him crazy at times. It was funny, he thought to himself, all the differences he found between Kay and Renee the more time he spent with her.

"Yeah, this cake is good. So what's been up, Renee?"

"Not too much . . . still looking for another job. I'm not sure how long A-Plus Advertising will stay in business."

"I heard TTA just laid off thirty of their employees," Kevin said.

"Yeah, and the rumor is that we're next."

"Damn, that must be rough. Job security is no joke . . . you gotta have it," Kevin said, concerned.

"I know, it's hard at times, but I love what I do and there are a lot of other companies out there that could use my expertise, so I'm not too worried. I just hope they give us enough notice if and when the time comes."

"Yeah . . . I hope so too," Kevin said.

"Phew . . . I'm stuffed!" Renee said, getting up. "Let me clean up this mess."

"You need some help?"

"That would be nice," Renee said sarcastically.

"Hey, watch it . . . not too many brothas that would offer to help clean up," Kevin said, defending himself.

"Well, I'll just consider myself lucky then," Renee said, smiling.

They headed toward the kitchen with empty boxes tucked everywhere.

"I can't believe we ate all this food," Renee said.

"That was you, 'Ms. Pit Bull,' eating all the chicken," Kevin said, laughing.

"Whatever, Kevin," Renee said, throwing the kitchen towel at him.

"Here, I'll wash and you dry . . . deal?"

"Deal."

The music stopped again.

"It looks like we went through another CD," Kevin said.

"I can't believe I stayed awake," Renee said, joking.

"What? With me around, you'll never want to sleep," Kevin said, bragging. The silence was welcome while they continued to clean the kitchen. It had been a long night. They were both exhausted from the key party.

"So it looks like we made it," Kevin said.

"Made what?"

"Made it through the night without making love," Kevin said, gazing into Renee's eyes.

"Oh . . . that."

"So, do we tell Nikki we bailed?" Kevin said, continuing to dry the dishes.

"Nah . . . let's tell her what she wants to hear."

"What . . . that we had wild-butt-naked sex till dawn?" Kevin said, breaking the tension.

"You're crazy," Renee said, smiling, a little disappointed that they didn't make love.

"Yeah, you're right, I *am* crazy. I can't believe I sat here with you all night and didn't get me some," Kevin said, laughing.

"You wouldn't know what to do with this anyway," Renee said.

"What? Is that a challenge?"

"No, Kevin . . . I was just kidding . . . damn."

"Oh, don't say shit you don't mean now, girl . . . 'cause Uncle Kevin will surely oblige."

"Oh, okay . . . Uncle Kevin . . . I'll keep that in mind," Renee said, splashing water at Kevin.

"Awww, you're in trouble now," Kevin said, filling up a cup of water.

"Kevin . . . don't play," Renee said, backing away. She ran over to the table and grabbed the can of whipped cream and got into her battle stance; she was ready to go to war if Kevin threw that water at her.

"Ohhhhhhh, you're playing dirty now," Kevin said, circling Renee with his cup of water.

"Kevin . . . Okay, I'll make a deal with you . . . I'll put the whipped cream down at the count of three as long as you do the same with that water. Deal?"

"Chicken!" Kevin said.

"One . . . two . . . three . . ." Neither of them stuck to the deal. Whipped cream and water went flying. "Ahhh ahhhhhhh . . . you cheater!" Renee screamed, dropping the can of whipped cream and running out of the kitchen.

"Me?" Kevin said. "You're the cheater. This was your rule . . . and now I look like Mr. Cool Whip himself."

"Haaaaaaaaa." Renee was cracking up. "I did kinda go crazy with the whipped cream. That's what you get . . . I told you not to mess with me."

"So, do you think I can get a towel?" Kevin said, licking the whipped cream off his fingers.

"Hmmmm, let me think about it," Renee joked.

Kevin couldn't help but notice how good she looked. Her red tank top was drenched and outlining the silhouette of her body perfectly. He could see her nipples poking out through her shirt, and her hair was sticking to her face. He walked over to her and moved the hair away from her eyes. Renee was still giggling at the sight of Kevin. His face was covered with whipped cream.

"Come on," Renee said.

"Where?"

"Let's go upstairs . . . you can take a shower . . . it's the least I could do since I got you all sticky," Renee said, with nothing but good intentions.

"Cool," Kevin said.

Renee took his hand and led him upstairs. Unfortunately, the only shower she had happened to be in her bedroom.

"Here's a towel and face cloth," Renee said, handing them to Kevin. "Let me know if you need anything else." He took the towel and wiped the whipped cream off his face.

"Actually I do," Kevin said, looking into Renee's pretty brown eyes.

"What?"

"Some company," Kevin said, taking her hand.

Renee thought her heart would pop right out of her chest. She didn't know what to do. Her shirt wasn't the only thing that was wet now.

"Stop playing, Kevin," she said, not knowing what else to say.

"I'm not."

Kevin was more serious than he'd been all night. He lifted his turtleneck over his head and dropped it onto the floor; his white tank top went with it.

Renee was stunned. His body looked as creamy as a Hershey's candy bar. He was in such good shape. She could count every ripple on his stomach. Her mind was spinning out of control, she couldn't think. She was breathing so hard she could barely speak. Then Kevin unbuttoned his pants and they dropped to the floor. White Calvin Klein boxers were all that were left. Renee didn't know quite what her next move should be, so she looked up at Kevin for guidance. He lifted her hands over her head and removed her red tank top and threw it on the bed. She wasn't wearing a bra. Her breasts were perfect. Her nipples were erect. She joined in and took her pants and panty hose off. Kevin couldn't help but stare at her beautiful naked body. He then walked toward the shower and turned the hot water on. Steam filled the bathroom. Kevin finished undressing and took Renee's hand and led her to the shower.

"Whoa . . . that's hot," Renee said, tilting her head back to let the water wet her hair.

Kevin loved Renee's long beautiful hair . . . the water straightened it, extending it just to the tip of her ass. She never looked more beautiful than she did at that moment. He took the shampoo and started to wash her hair, then his. Renee watched as the soap streamed down his chiseled body.

"Could you wash my back?" Kevin said to her, handing her the soapy washrag.

Renee didn't say a word. She just took the washcloth from him and started to wash his entire body. He turned around and took her hand and led it down his stomach. She was so turned on. She stroked him up and down and up and down. She wanted him bad as hell and she could tell that he wanted her too.

"Kevin?"

"Yeah?"

"Do you wanna know what I was going to say earlier when we were dancing?"

"Yes."

"I was going to ask you to make love to me."

"You were?"

"Yes . . . I was."

"And now?"

"Now I'm sure that's what I want you to do."

Kevin wasted no time. He turned off the water and opened the shower door. He and Renee stepped out. He grabbed the towel she gave him and patted her dry.

"I've wanted to kiss you all night," he said, taking her face in his arms. Renee closed her eyes, inviting him to kiss her, then . . .

. . . *Knock . . . knock . . . knock!*

"Renee?"

"Oh my God, it's Jason," Renee said, breaking from Kevin's arms in a panic.

"What the hell is he doing here?" Kevin said, pissed.

"I don't know," Renee said, almost relieved that Jason had interrupted things with Kevin. "Hurry up, Kevin . . . put your clothes on . . . he cannot find us up here," she said, scurrying around to find something to put on. She grabbed her Gap jeans lying on the bed and threw a sweatshirt on. She pulled her hair back in a ponytail and stuck it in a bun in an attempt to hide the fact that her hair was wet. Kevin had already gotten dressed and just watched as Renee transformed herself into another person right before his eyes.

"I don't get it. What's the big deal? He knew you were supposed to be here with someone, right? I mean . . . he did agree to the key party, didn't he?" Kevin said, waiting for an explanation for Renee's behavior.

"You don't understand, Kevin. He can't find us up here. Come on, let's go back downstairs. I'll explain later, okay?" Renee said, making sure her room was exactly how she left it.

Knock . . . knock . . . knock!

"Renee, I know you're in there!" Jason screamed. He was drunk and loud. A few of the neighbors' lights came on, which clued him to be a little more inconspicuous.

Renee darted down the steps and hurriedly ran to the front door, slinging it open.

"Jason? What are you doing here?" she said, trying to control her breathing. Kevin had already made it down the steps and was sitting on the sofa, mad as hell. Not only was he extremely disappointed, he was pissed at the way Renee was acting. He didn't like to see her like this . . . it made him uneasy. Why was she so afraid? he thought to himself. And what the hell was Jason doing here? *Damn!*

"I . . . I'm sorry, Renee," Jason said, walking through the front door. "I tried to hurry."

"Jason, you're not making any sense. Tried to hurry for what? You knew where I would be tonight and you knew what I would be doing."

"I know. That's what I mean . . . I tried to hurry and stop you," Jason continued. "Am I too late?"

"Too late for what?" Renee was confused.

"Did you *fuck* him?" Jason said, noticing Kevin for the first time. "*Oh . . . ain't this shit convenient?*" Jason yelled. "*Did you pick her key on purpose, maaan? Get out . . . get the fuck out,*" Jason screamed. He could have handled anyone else but Kevin being there at that moment. He always knew deep down that Kevin and Renee had a thing for each other. Not just from the spin-the-bottle incident, but even after that. He would notice Kevin checking her out when he thought no one else was looking, and he definitely saw it in Renee's eyes whenever Kevin would come around.

Kevin stood up and walked over to Jason.

"Look, Jay, man, you're trippin. Now, I don't know what the hell is going on here, but I do know this . . . you're drunk and you better believe I'm not leaving until you calm your ass down."

Kevin was heated. Jason was his friend, but he wasn't thinking about anyone else but Renee right now. And he didn't feel right about leaving her with Jason in his condition.

"Kevin . . . it's okay . . . .please just go . . . you're going to make it worse if you stay," Renee said, upset.

"Renee, what's going on?" Kevin said, taking his attention away from Jason for a moment. "Didn't he know about this?"

"I'll explain later, Kevin . . . just go . . . please . . . just go," Renee pleaded.

"Look, man . . . she doesn't have to explain shit to you . . . you're not her man . . . you may wish you were . . . but you're not . . . so step before I make you regret coming here tonight," Jason said, enraged.

"You threatening me?" Kevin said, getting in Jason's face.

"Stop it!" Renee said, stepping between Jason and Kevin. She grabbed Kevin's hand and dragged him to the door. "Kevin, please go home. I promise I'll be all right . . . I promise."

"How can I leave you like this, Renee?"

"Trust me, Kevin . . . just go . . . I'll be fine. I'll explain everything later. I promise."

Kevin looked in her teary brown eyes and decided to go. He felt uncomfortable as hell leaving, but he convinced himself that Renee knew what she was talking about.

"All right, I'll go, but let me holla at Jay for a second."

"No . . . leave him alone, Kevin . . . he's not going to listen to you right now."

"Renee, I'm not leaving until I say something to this fool. He's tripping and I'm not leaving until he calms his ass down."

"He's already calmer now that he knows you're leaving. Just go, Kevin . . . go."

"Renee, I'm not leaving until I talk to him." Kevin carefully moved Renee out of the way and went toward the living room.

"Hey, Jason . . . look, man . . . I don't know what's got you all up in arms tonight . . . but just know this . . . I didn't cross any lines . . . as far as I knew, this was a game and we were all in on it . . . so I'll leave under one condition . . . you calm down and look me in the eye and tell me that you and Renee are cool."

Jason had calmed down considerably since he first stepped through the door.

"I'm cool, Kevin . . . no hard feelings, right? I'm straight . . . really . . . you can go."

Against Kevin's better judgment he decided to leave.

Renee walked him to the door. She was flushed and obviously upset.

"Look, Renee . . . I still don't feel right about this."

"You're doing the right thing Kevin . . . it was a great night . . . let's leave it at that," Renee said, sad to see Kevin go.

Kevin looked back at Renee on his way to the parking lot. He was a little choked up himself. He'd had a great night and hated to see it end. He felt like this was the last time he was ever going to see her. He never did get that kiss he was waiting for all night and now he knew he never would. As he stepped into his Suburban he noticed a little white piece of paper stuck to the bottom of his shoe. He pulled it off. It was the fortune that Renee had fought so hard to keep away from him. It read . . . *Your destiny is staring you in the face.*

Twelve

Ladies' Talk

Nikki couldn't even concentrate at work. The party had finally come and gone and she hadn't talked to anyone or heard anything about how things went. The girls were finally all going to meet up tonight so they could see each other face-to-face and talk about it all. She couldn't wait to leave. She hadn't even seen or talked to Lynda since their night together. All she could think about was how Lynda had gone out on a limb and uncovered some very true feelings. It hadn't been half bad, though, Nikki thought to herself, smiling a little. She didn't regret anything. She could openly and honestly say that much. She felt that she had done something that most friends couldn't do. That most friends, in fact, wouldn't do. She had given herself to Lynda because she knew that's what her friend needed most. The last thing Lynda had needed that night was to be judged, or even worse, rejected. Lynda was looking for answers that night, and Nikki was able to allow Lynda to answer questions she had probably been asking herself for years. And Nikki felt good about that. What she felt a little uncomfortable with was having lied to Chris. Well, not exactly lied, but she conveniently left out information about that night.

When Chris had come home that night, after he and Jason talked at the hotel, he assumed that because Jason didn't have a partner, his partner was supposed to be Nikki and that something just kind of got screwed up. Nikki knew that Chris found comfort in knowing that by luck of the draw, Nikki had missed out on the festivities completely.

When he came into the house he said he thought he had seen Lynda pass him, but he couldn't really tell since her windows were tinted. Nikki told him that he had, in fact, seen Lynda and that she had come over to tell Nikki that she chickened out of the whole thing. She had grabbed Nikki's key by accident in an attempt to take her own key out of the drawing. She didn't have the nerve to tell everyone, so she tried to do it secretly. This was what Nikki told Chris. She wasn't proud of it, but she thought it was in his best interest to have this be his truth of what had happened that night.

She was getting ready to leave work to go and meet the girls at a restaurant near the health club where she and Lynda used to work out together. She didn't know what to expect of everyone and didn't really know what they expected her to say. They weren't supposed to talk about what had happened the other night in too much detail. They would all be pissed to find out that Chris and Jason didn't sleep with anyone because Lynda screwed everything up. She just figured she would think of something to say when it was time.

* * *

Lynda was sitting on her bed looking through old pictures of her and Rick, drinking a glass of wine. She looked over at the clock. It was already five o'clock. She was meeting the girls at six o'clock, so she decided to go ahead and put something on so she could go. She looked a real mess. She had been crying all day. Between the time she had left Nikki's house the other night after the key party and her pulling up into her own driveway she had made a major decision. She was leaving Rick. She couldn't live the lie any longer. Not to herself and definitely not to Rick. He was a good man and he deserved a good woman who was going to love him back the way he needed to be loved.

She had tried to convince herself throughout their marriage that she could be a good woman to Rick. But now she knew she couldn't and she had to do the right thing. She changed into some black pants and a top and threw on her black boots and left. She didn't know how to tell the girls. She wasn't ready to tell them she was a lesbian. She decided she would tell them about her decision to end her marriage and just to leave it at that for now. What would she do now, though? Where would she live? How would her life end up? These were all questions she knew she wouldn't be able to answer right away. The first step was finding the strength to tell Rick.

Kay was leaving the gym, getting ready to go meet the girls. She needed to work out the stress she was feeling from her night with Rick. She couldn't believe she was capable of having such passion with another man. She didn't feel guilty, really, just overwhelmed. She wondered how she would face Rick again without thinking about that night. Would she be attracted to him now? Or was it just the key party that sparked their desires? She wondered what Rick was thinking. When he left her place that night, they had kissed gently on the lips and sworn that they would never discuss what happened with a soul. They each thanked the other for a great night and he left. She wondered how she would be satisfied sexually without ever doing the things she and Rick experienced. The workout helped clear her mind. She decided that she was going to do what she and Rick said. Never discuss it with a soul. Not one living soul. She had already showered and was picking up her ID from the front window and returning her towels. The gentleman standing in line ahead of her was finishing up. When he turned around he bumped right into her, knocking all of the things she was holding to the floor.

"Damn," Kay said, rolling her eyes. The guy was already trying to help her pick up her belongings. When she looked up she realized that she knew him. Her expression totally changed.

"Brian?"

"Yeah, I'm Brian."

"I'm Kay. I showed you a house about two weeks ago. The five-bedroom over there off of West Paces Ferry?"

"Oh yeah. How are you?"

"I'm fine. Just trying to stay in some kind of shape, you know."

"You seem to be doing okay with that," Brian said, smiling slyly.

"Do you work around here?" Kay asked him.

"Um, yeah, well, no, I . . . I." Brian was stuttering over his words. "I sort of have a confession," he told Kay.

"Confession?" she asked, puzzled.

"Hey, do you have some time now? We could go grab some coffee or something next door," Brian said.

Kay looked at her watch and saw that it was five-fifteen. She had about thirty minutes to kill.

"Maybe another time?" Brian said. "You look worried and I don't want to make you late for your next stop."

"No," Kay said. "Let's go."

When they sat down at the coffee shop, Kay noticed how handsome Brian really was. His complexion was beautiful and he had great eyes. He seemed really nice. Kay had a sudden thought that brought her back to reality. What if he was crazy? she thought for a brief moment before he started talking.

"So this is the deal, Kay, and I'm only telling you this because I like your smile," he said, nodding.

Kay started to blush unknowingly.

"I'm not really in the market for a house. I was kind of sent to find you."

"Sent to find me?"

"Yeah. I work for your company's competitor," Brian told her, "Lomax. The word around our office is that your signs are starting to appear in more and more front yards around town. You're the best there is, from what I've been told. I just set up our little meeting so I could feel you out, so to speak," he said, leaning up in his chair.

"Oh, really?" Kay said.

"You see," Brian said, "I'm the best at what I do in my office as well. And I wanted to learn a little more about my archrival."

It all started to make sense. Kay knew that Brian seemed familiar for some reason. "You're Brian Carter, aren't you?" Kay asked.

"Yes, ma'am," he said.

"I've seen your signs around, too," Kay told him. "I thought you looked familiar that day I was showing the house, but you had on a hat and I couldn't put it together. You sneaky bastard!" she said out loud.

"Oh, c'mon, Kay, you can't blame a man for wanting to see you up close and personal. It was nothing personal," Brian said. "Friends?" he said, reaching his hand out toward Kay's.

She shook it hesitantly.

"In fact, since that day I've been thinking about some things that we could talk about . . . but another time because you obviously have to go."

"Brian, I'm sorry, I do have to go and I'm involved with someone anyway."

"Oh no, I'm sorry," Brian said. "I'm a happily married man. I have been for twelve years. What I want to talk to you about is business related."

Kay wanted to die right there.

"Here's my card," Brian said. "Please call me, I really think we should talk."

"Okay, Brian, I'll call you sometime next week then," Kay said.

"Take care, Kay," he said. "And slow down," he told her, waving as she walked out the door.

Nikki pulled up to the restaurant and saw Lynda's car behind her. They parked near each other and walked in together. They saw Renee at a table near the middle of the place and walked over.

"Hey, Renee," Nikki said, taking off her coat and sitting down. She looked so tired, Nikki thought, or maybe it was nervous energy that she felt around the table instead.

"Where is Kay?" Nikki and Lynda asked.

"She just called me. She's running a little late and made me promise we wouldn't talk about anything major until she got here."

"She's funny," Lynda said.

While they were giving their drink order, Kay walked up hurriedly.

"Did I miss anything?" she asked, huffing and puffing.

"No, we've only been here like ten minutes," Renee said.

"Cool, well, hi, everyone," Kay said, realizing she had just blown in right in the middle of a discussion.

"We were just about to start catching up," Nikki said. "I was reminding everyone that we cannot give away any names here about what happened the other night after we left the party. Remember, we all promised."

"I wish I hadn't promised," Kay said, "because I would love to know which one of you got a taste of my Kevin."

"I know," Nikki said, "but a promise is a promise. Besides, that would be too much to handle if we all started telling each other how great the sex was with our significant others, don't you think?"

"I didn't do it," Lynda said out of the blue.

Nikki looked astonished.

"What do you mean you didn't do it?" Renee said, putting her drink down.

"I didn't go through with the key-party thing. Not the right way."

"Um . . ." Nikki jumped in. "She didn't have the guts

to do it, so she took her key out of the bowl. She didn't want anyone to pull her key, you know. But she actually pulled my key, instead," Nikki told them.

"What?" Kay said.

"Yeah," Lynda said, "that's exactly what happened."

Nikki patted Lynda's knee gently under the table to let her know it was okay.

"So, what does that mean?" Kay said.

"What it means is that two out of the four guys didn't go through with this thing," Nikki said.

"The question is, which two?" Renee said.

"You know, don't you, Nikki?" Kay said, pointing at Nikki.

"Why do you think I know?" Nikki asked, trying to put on her best poker face.

"Because I bet Chris pulled Lynda's key and went to her house and found out she either wasn't there or had decided against this whole thing."

"Whatever," Nikki said to Kay, "you think you're so smart."

"Let's not argue," Renee said, "it's pointless. It's over now."

"Look," Nikki said, getting pissed, "I didn't come here to be attacked. I can leave for all this fucking drama."

"No," Lynda said, "don't leave. I think everyone is still a bit surprised that all of this happened period."

"I'm sorry," Kay said, apologizing to Nikki.

Renee kept sipping on her drink.

"Well, I went through with it," Kay said.

"So did I," Renee said. "Sort of."

"What do you mean, sort of?" Nikki asked.

"Well, Jason came and interrupted everything."

"Jason?" Lynda said. "Why wasn't he at someone's house doing his own thing?"

"I don't know," Renee said. "Maybe he got screwed out of it, when you took Nikki's key."

"Oh," Lynda said, looking down.

"Or, maybe he just finished early with his person, I don't know. He didn't come home until late," Renee said. "But anyway, he came to my house all in a rage and ruined everything. My patience has grown so thin with him I don't know what to do at this point."

"That boy needs some counseling," Kay said.

"I agree," Nikki and Lynda both said.

"Yeah, I think he and I need to have a long talk sometime this week, because I just can't go on if some things don't change, and I mean quick," Renee said.

"I'm having a talk with Rick too," Lynda said. "I'm going to tell him that I'm leaving him."

Kay started choking on her wine, and Renee had half a quesadilla hanging out of her mouth and was trying to put it down. Nikki knew why, but was still very surprised to hear that Lynda had made the decision so quickly.

Nikki jumped in. "Why, Lynda? What happened? Please tell me it wasn't because of the key party."

She was *such* the little actress, Lynda thought to herself.

"No, Nikki," Lynda said. "It wasn't the key party. In fact, this party showed me more about myself than I was willing to see most of my life. I just know that Rick and I will never make each other as happy as we both deserve to be, that's all."

"That's it?" Kay said. "That's all you have to say about a man you've been married to for ten years?"

"Well, of course not," Lynda said, "but it's all you need to hear. I just wanted to tell you guys before I told him because I know I'm going to need some support after this goes down. I don't think he'll take it well. I mean, I've been his everything for all these years and I know this is going to crush him."

They all kind of sat back in their chairs and stared off into space.

"Wow," Renee said. "This is all so wild. Lynda is leaving Rick and Jason is crazy as hell. It seems the only two couples that have it all in line are you guys," she said, referring to Nikki's and Kay's relationships. Renee knew that the statement she made wasn't completely true, but she had to say it.

"I'm sorry to hear what you're going through, Lynda," Renee said. "I really am. But we'll be here for you no matter what, okay?" She stood up and gave Lynda a hug.

They all had tears in their eyes. They agreed to try and put the party behind them and not continue to probe each other for more details. The party was over and they had all decided to accept things for what they were. It just wasn't time for all truths to be told that day.

"So when do you plan to tell him?" Renee asked Lynda.

"Tomorrow, I think. I don't want to drag it out any longer than I have to."

"Then what?" Kay asked.

"Great question, Kay, and if I had the answer to that one I guess my life would be just perfect," Lynda said. "I have no idea what will be next for me. I guess we'll sell the house and I'll get my own place. Luckily, I have a good bit of money saved up so that won't be an issue for me. More than anything, I think I'll just spend the next year trying to figure myself out. I'll probably end up moving out West, though. I could make so much more money in personal training. People out there are much more concerned about their appearance."

"So, does this mean that we can't hang out with you and Rick anymore?" Nikki asked. "I mean, Chris and Rick are best friends."

"I really don't want it to be that way," Lynda said. "It's going to be weird for a while, though. It's going to take some adjusting for all of us since Rick and I share all the same friends. I'm going to miss that part of what Rick and I were. The part that included all of you. But I know one thing. I won't miss my mother-in-law one bit. That bitch used to talk me to damn death."

All the girls laughed together, slapping each other five. Life had changed for all of them, but they would get through it. Somehow they were all pretty sure of that.

"Well, I hate to bust this party up, but I need to go home to my husband and see how he's doing," Nikki said. "He hasn't said too much about the party either."

"Yeah, I haven't talked to Kevin about it yet," Kay said.

"I'm going home to think about what to say to Jason," Renee said. "I hate to have to give him an ultimatum, but I don't think I have a choice. He has got to make some serious changes or I will be single next year."

"Well, let's try to get together again next week, ladies," Nikki said, putting on her coat.

"Cool," Kay and Renee said.

"That'll work," Lynda said. "I should be in a better state of mind by then."

They settled the bill and walked out to the parking lot together.

"Group hug?" Nikki asked.

"You are such drama," Kay told her, giving them all a hug.

"Love you guys," Nikki said, getting in her car.

"All right, love you too," Renee said.

"Me too," Lynda said.

"Me three," Kay said, waving good-bye.

Thirteen

Chris and Nikki

Nikki cried most of the way home. She felt so bad for what Lynda was going through. She felt some comfort that the key party wasn't to blame for Lynda and Rick's breakup. She didn't know how it had affected the other girls, but figured it was just too soon after everything had happened to ask too many questions. She wanted to talk to Chris. She wanted to see what info he had gotten, if any, from the guys. She hoped it wouldn't be worse than what the girls were going through.

When she pulled into her driveway she took a moment to clean up her face and get herself together. She didn't want Chris to know how distraught she was over everything. She grabbed her purse and went into the house. The TV was off in the living room and there was no sign of Chris. She knew he was home, because his truck was in the driveway. She went into the kitchen and everything was just as she had left it. Where was Chris? she thought. She started walking upstairs just wanting to lie down and forget about everything for a moment.

When she opened her bedroom door she was completely surprised. There had to be damn near fifty candles lit all over the place. Chris was lying on the bed in his boxers looking sexy as hell. He had cooked her chicken stir-fry and had it hot and ready to serve. There were two bottles of wine on their small table near the window. Two glasses were already poured.

"What are you doing, Chris?" Nikki asked. She was smiling and had finally made her way over to the bed, dropping her purse on the floor. Chris got up and walked over to her side of the bed.

"You look so tired, baby. Let me help you relax." As he started to undress her, she started to fight a little to keep her clothes on. She just wasn't in the mood tonight.

"No, baby, it's not about that. Just let me do this, okay?" Chris told her.

Nikki took a deep breath and allowed him to undress her. She wasn't sure what he had up his sleeve. He picked her up and walked toward their bathroom. There were just as many candles surrounding their garden tub and there were flower petals floating on top of the bubbles in the water. He knelt down and slowly lowered Nikki into the hot bath he had drawn for her. Nikki closed her eyes and let Chris take over. This was just what she needed.

"Chris, you're so—"

"Shhhh . . ." he interrupted. He got up for a second and came back with two bobby pins and started pinning her hair up so it wouldn't get wet. He lifted up one of her legs and ran hot sudsy water down it and watched as she just took it all in. She was up to her neck in bubbles and flowers and he thought she had never looked more beautiful. He leaned over and gave her a full kiss on the lips.

"I want to talk to you about something," Chris told Nikki. "And I don't want you to talk, I just want you to listen."

She nodded her head, letting him know that she would not interrupt.

"We've been married for six years now, Nikki, and it's been better than anything I could possibly have imagined. I never had a doubt that you were the woman God made for me. You're my wife, my lover, my partner, and most importantly, my friend. There's nothing I wouldn't do for you, and I want you to know and believe that with all your heart. But now there's something I need you to do for me. I never thought I'd be able to love a woman as much as I love you. And what's scary is that there's even more love that I have to give to you. The thing I liked most about you when we were dating was your carefree way about life. You were always the one trying to get the most out of life for yourself and for those closest to you. Your open-mindedness is probably scary to most people, but that's one of the things that really attracted me to you. The key party is just an example of your willingness to try new things and to constantly grow within yourself, unafraid. But I'm asking you to put that part of you on hold for a little while." Chris had been speaking so deeply that he didn't even realize that Nikki had started to cry.

"Looking back on this year, Nikki, I see how blessed we've been. We have great jobs, great friends, and all the things that go along with those. We have a beautiful house, we're both able to buy the things we want, clothes, cars, et cetera. But what's the point of having all of that

and keeping it for just the two of us? I love you with all
that I am, Nikki, and I guess what I'm asking you is this.
Would you have our baby?"

At that moment Nikki broke down and started bawl-
ing. She sat up in the tub and buried her face in her
hands.

"What is it, baby? Did I say something wrong?"

"No, Chris, of course not. You're such a great husband. Just listening to you say all those beautiful things
made me realize that I would never want to lose you or
for you to feel like I take you for granted. I'm so fortu-
nate to have a good man who wants to give me the
world. I just want to love you forever. Yes, Chris, I would
love to start a family with you," Nikki said, giggling
slightly. The idea of it made her smile and feel warm all
over. "There's nothing better I can think of doing than
putting all of my energy into you and our baby," she
told him. Chris started smiling then.

"All right!" he yelled. "So what do you say we get
started now?" he asked her with a sly look on his face.

"Come here, boy," Nikki said, grabbing him around
his neck and pulling him into the water. They both
started laughing at the big splash they'd made and all
the water that had flowed over onto the bathroom
floor. Nikki started to get up to clean it up.

"Not now," Chris told her, "we have more important
things to do."

They started to kiss in a way that made Nikki never
want to stop. She had put all the stress and tears behind
her now. She was with Chris now, and once again, he
had made everything all right.

Fourteen

Jason and Renee

Renee was the first one to arrive at the office Monday morning. She'd had a pretty quiet night, just reflecting on the talk she'd had with the girls. She was up all night reviewing a huge PowerPoint presentation she had to finish up for a prospective client; and she had come in early to get a head start. If she landed the JazzDigital account, her life would never be the same. Sharp's Advertising was just one of twelve advertising agencies lined up to present to JazzDigital today, and quiet as it was kept Renee didn't think her agency had a chance. It was a much smaller agency than Berk's or even P & E Advertising. They would have to lease another space to accommodate the number of executives needed to handle the JazzDigital account. Jill Smith, president of Sharp's Advertising, was more than ready to do just that.

The pressure was on and Renee didn't feel as prepared as she should. Out of the six account executives in the office, Jill chose Renee to present to JazzDigital. It was the chance of a lifetime, but all Renee could think about was Saturday night and Kevin. That had been one of the best and worst nights of her life. The best being Kevin, wet, soapy, and looking so fine in her shower; the worst being Jason interrupting that long-awaited kiss. She could still feel Kevin's arms around her. She tried her hardest to get him out of her mind, her heart, out of her soul. She must have replayed that night in her head a million times. She studied every inch of him in her mind as she drifted off into a daydream.

How could I want Kevin so bad? she asked herself. She never thought that a simple attraction would turn into such passion. *What are these feelings? Lust? Obsession?* Then she hesitated . . . *Love? Nah* . . . she couldn't let herself go there. *That's crazy*, she told herself. *I love Jason*, she thought convincingly. But Renee wasn't convinced at all, especially after what had happened on Saturday night. Not just with Kevin, but with Jason. He'd been acting so insane lately. Lashing out at the craziest things. She couldn't figure out what was going on with him. He wouldn't talk to her. All he did lately was yell at her and then apologize later. He was like two different people. That's why she was having a hard time letting him go. At one moment, he was the Jason she had fallen in love with. Those hazel eyes of his were all she could think of when she first laid eyes on him. His smile was warm and inviting and he was always a little shy. She always knew that there was something beneath the surface. The panic attacks he would have once in a while, the bad nightmares that woke him out of a deep sleep with no explanation. She tried to talk to him about his childhood several times, but he would always clam up or change the subject. She even suggested therapy once, but he blew up at her, saying he wasn't crazy; but he was sure acting crazy.

They had had a long talk after Kevin left that night. And even though he apologized for screaming at her and Kevin, she never sensed that he was truly sorry. He even tried to make love to her and when she resisted he got angry all over again. He accused her of wanting Kevin instead. She denied it, of course, but deep down she knew Jason was right. Part of her did want Kevin that night and still wanted him. She felt guilty as hell, but she couldn't control it. She and Kevin had reached a forbidden level that night that couldn't be denied. She wondered if Kevin was thinking of her, too. She had visions of him going home to Kay that night and making love to her, pretending it was Renee. She felt pretty guilty about that, especially the part of her that felt some happiness that he might be pretending, but what if he wasn't pretending with Kay? What if it was her that he was pretending with? *Damn, I have to stop obsessing about this man and get to work,* she thought. Just then her coworker Charlene walked in.

"Hey, Renee, you're here early."

"Good morning, Charlene. I know, I got here around six a.m You know I have this presentation with JazzDigital today at three."

"Damn, I don't envy you, are you ready for it?"

"Nope!"

"Really? Do you need some help?"

"No, I just need to brush up on my Billboard knowledge. I wanna be able to answer every question they throw at me."

"Well, at least Rhonda will be there . . . that bitch is the best bullshitter I know," Charlene said.

"Yeah, I know, she and David should have my back with the copywriting and creative issues. I just need to present a strong case on what I can do for them. I need to get my head right. We definitely need to show a united front, being such a small agency. That's the first thing they're going to ask us, is how we plan on catering to all of their divisions, being solely based in Atlanta. I wish they would regionalize this shit. These national companies kill me trying to have just one agency. I mean, it would be so much better for them to have an agency in each market."

"Yeah, Cassandra about died when she lost Raytheon to those bigwigs in New York. Her commission dropped about fifty percent."

"Ooooh, I know, that was ugly," Renee said, feeling more pressure than ever. "And you know what I hate the most about this? I'm the only AE presenting. I still think they should have had you and maybe even Cassandra presenting with me. I think that would be a lot more convincing to them. They're going to be looking at me like, 'What's she going to do with all of this?'"

"Well, that's when you step up and talk about the team of AEs you have behind you. You can do it, girl. Jill wouldn't have picked you if she didn't think you could do it."

"I know I can, I just had a crazy weekend, that's all, and I didn't really spend the time I should have spent on this. I planned on working on this all day yesterday, but I didn't get around to it. Jason was over and I spent the entire day nursing a couple of wounds."

"What's going on with you and Jason?"

"Nothing I really have time to go into right now, just drama. I gotta get this going, Charlene, so I'll talk to you later."

"Okay, Renee . . . I need to get to work my damn self. Keep your head up, okay?"

"I will, thanks, Charlene."

Renee closed her office door and finished up her presentation. She didn't take a lunch and by the time she looked up it was two o'clock. She felt pretty confident that she would walk into JazzDigital's corporate office and do the best job she could. She knew that landing the account would be a long shot, but she was going to put her best foot forward and give it her all.

Jason was just getting out of the shower when he heard the phone ring. It was Chris.

"What's up, Jay?"

"Hey, Chris."

"I called your office but they said you hadn't made it in yet. You okay?"

"Yeah, I'm cool, I just had a long day yesterday so I slept in. I'm up now, getting ready to go in."

"So . . . how did it go on Saturday? Did you get to Renee in time?"

"Yeah, just in the nick of time apparently. Kevin was there looking all pissed like I interrupted something."

"Oh, word? So Kevin picked Renee, huh? Damn!"

"Yeah, damn. And she had the nerve to look disappointed to see me too."

"Well, what went down?"

"Maaan, I tripped a little, you know me . . . I was drunk and started yelling. Kevin tried to get all up in my face like he was defending his woman. I wanted to beat his ass just for being there, but I managed to calm down and remembered that it was my own damn fault. I never should have told Renee that I would do this."

"Maan, don't even front, Jay . . . you were down as hell until you ended up without a key. Ha, ha."

"Ha, ha . . . yeah, you're right. I'm not gonna lie, I

was ready to wax somebody's ass that night. It would have made all the difference if I had. I think I really screwed up this time. Renee was looking at me like the devil all day yesterday."

"Oh, really, you stayed the night?"

"More like I passed out and Renee threw a blanket over my drunk behind and went to bed."

"Damn, Jay, you were pretty drunk when I left you, but I thought the ride over would have chilled you out a bit."

"Well, I was straight until I saw Kevin. I don't know what's up with her and Kevin, but that muthafucka checks her out every chance he gets. He doesn't know that I know, but trust me, I can tell."

"What? I don't think so, man. Kevin and Kay seem pretty tight to me. I mean, if he's checking Renee out it's probably because she looks just like his babe. That's gotta be weird as hell. I mean, I can't imagine someone who looked just like Nikki being in our crew. That twin shit is crazy. I mean, they look exactly the same," Chris said.

"Naaaah, I can tell them apart easy. The funny thing is, and this is going to trip you out, Kay is actually finer than Renee."

"What? That's crazy. I mean, Kay might show her ass a little more than Renee, but it's the same ass, I don't care what you say, Jay."

"Trust me, Kay is finer. It's very subtle but you can tell when you're dating one of them. I mean, it's impossible to not tell. I've studied them over this past year and I'm telling you, they are both fine as hell, but Kay has a little more of something. I think it's because Kay is more outgoing than Renee is. I mean, Renee is mostly about work and Kay is mostly about play. And play always looks better than work."

"Okay, okay . . . I'm feeling you a little now. Kay is definitely sexier. But they're both fine as hell. That shit is equal."

"Ha, ha . . . yeah, I know. And to tell you the truth, I could never be with Kay. She's a little too wild for me," Jason said. "What if I would have picked her key? That shit would have been sweet, ha, ha."

"Yeah," Chris said. "That definitely would have been interesting. So, what's up, man, you think you guys are going to be okay?"

"Well, I'm going to see if I can smooth some shit over today. She has this big presentation to do today, so I thought I would surprise her."

"Surprise her with what?"

"I have a little something in the works. Trust me, she'll be pleased!"

"That's cool. Well, call me and let me know how it goes. Oh, so what about you and Kevin? Y'all straight?" Chris asked, concerned.

"Yeah, me and Kevin will always be straight. He left on a good note. It may be a little awkward the next time I see him, but we'll be cool by the time the next card game comes around."

"Cool. As a matter of fact, I'll go ahead and start setting that up. I'll holla at ya later, Jay."

"All right, Chris, Peace."

Jason felt much better having spoken to Chris. Their talks had really helped Jason, whether Chris knew it or not. Jason started to imagine what his night was going to be like with Renee. He had some real sucking up to do. He showed out on Saturday and things weren't any better on Sunday. When he woke up and found himself on the couch Sunday morning, he accused Renee of all types of crazy things. He asked her if she dreamt about Kevin all night, he asked her if her pussy got wet thinking about Kevin. He was out of control with jealously; Renee never answered him. She just looked at him with rage and contempt. "How could I be with this man?" was all Jason saw in her teary eyes. He really let her down. He left her on Sunday, promising that he would get his act together. She wouldn't even let him kiss her good-bye. It devastated him, but deep down he knew he deserved it. But he was going to make it up to her tonight if it killed him. He still wanted to know what had happened between her and Kevin on Saturday. It was eating him up inside. Did they have sex? Was that what he had interrupted? Renee wouldn't answer any of his questions and it was driving him crazy. Why? Why wasn't she answering him? Was she guilty of something? She had to be. He truly felt that it had been more than just a game for her and Kevin and that perhaps she felt guilty about it deep down inside and that's why she couldn't talk to him about it. "Ahhhhh," Jason screamed. "Get your shit together, Jay," he continued preaching to himself. "You have her. She plans on marrying your crazy ass and you're blowing it. You can't lose her, you can't." He started to tear up a bit. He was so messed up inside emotionally and he wanted so badly to heal, but he didn't know how, and he knew he couldn't even begin to heal without Renee in his life. He vowed to make things right again. "Tonight will be a whole new beginning for me and Renee," he said out loud to himself. He left his house with a renewed sense of confidence for once. He wouldn't mess this up no matter what.

* * *

Five o'clock could not have come any sooner for Renee when she left JazzDigital's corporate office and headed back to the office. The presentation went great; Renee put on the performance of a lifetime. Jill, Leeann, and Peter marveled at her professionalism and confidence. There wasn't a question the CEO threw at her that she wasn't fully prepared to answer. He even complimented her on her Chanel suit. She felt 100 percent when she got in her car and headed back to the office. She planned on leaving a little earlier today, but still had a few loose ends to tie up before she left the office. She called and left a message for her dad to let him know how things had turned out. He had been helping her keep her sanity through it all, reminding her that he had raised an intelligent and confident woman. He would be so proud of her.

She hadn't spoken to Jason all day and felt at peace for once. He was stressing her out immensely lately and she welcomed the break. She was used to talking to him every day. She was surprised and a little hurt, though, that he hadn't at least called to wish her good luck. But she made it through anyway and wondered if that was why she did so well. His voice might have put her in a totally different mood. The difference between this morning and many other before was that she had peace of mind. And it really felt nice.

She couldn't remember the last time they'd had a normal conversation without arguing. All she wanted to do was go home, take a hot bath, eat some leftover Chinese food, and curl up with a good book.

When she finally did reach her driveway, the sight of

Jason's car parked in front of her apartment was more than surprising. "Damn it," she said, disappointed to see that he was there. "I'm so not in the mood for this shit tonight," Renee continued as she placed her head down on the steering wheel. She needed to mentally prepare herself to see him. *What the hell is he doing here?* she thought. She was a little surprised that he had the nerve to use the key she had given him so long ago, when things were good between them. How dare he take advantage of her giving him that key now of all times? What was he thinking? she thought.

Renee lifted her head and pulled herself together. When she walked through the door Jason was walking down the stairs looking as fine as ever. He had on a crisp white linen shirt tucked into the khaki slacks she'd bought him the previous year. His hair was cut low like she loved it and he had shaved for the first time in weeks. *He's so damn pretty with his high-yellow self,* Renee thought. His hazel eyes glistened as he approached her with a warm smile.

"Hi, honey, welcome home," he said, kissing her softly on her cheek.

Renee's eyes were filled with tears of joy, yet guilt for the horrible thoughts that had gone through her mind earlier.

"What's wrong?" Jason asked her.

"Nothing. What are you doing here? And why are you so dressed up?"

"I left work early today. I wanted to surprise you and celebrate your success with the JazzDigital account."

"Success?"

"Yes, the presentation you did today?"

"Oh, that? Ha, ha . . . how do you know I was successful?"

"Because I know you can do anything you set your mind to do and I knew that you would wow them and I was right, right?"

"Well, yeah, I was pretty impressive, if I do say so myself," and they both started to laugh. The sound of the two of them laughing felt so good to Renee at that moment. She and Jason had done nothing but fight for the last couple of weeks. The tension had been thick, but not tonight. When she walked into her living room she walked right back into his heart. Kevin wasn't gone from her thoughts completely, but neatly tucked away for now.

Just then there was a knock on the door. Renee looked at Jason, puzzled.

"Who could that be?" she asked him.

"I don't know, why don't you answer it and find out?"

"What are you up to?" she said, smiling, not being able to take her eyes off Jason as she approached the door. To her surprise a chauffeur was standing on her front porch when she opened the door. He had on a black hat, tux, and the whole nine. When he stepped to the side she saw the most beautiful black stretch Lexus limousine she'd ever seen. She was floored.

She turned and asked Jason, "What's going on?"

"Why don't you go upstairs and get dressed?" Jason said, pleased with himself.

"Dressed? Why? Where are we going?" Renee asked with a big grin on her face. Jason was always good for being elaborate. She loved that about him. The last few weeks were slowly drifting out of her mind as she dashed upstairs to get ready. When she reached her bedroom a huge package with a big red bow sat pretty in the middle of her bed. Renee's face lit up! She quickly unwrapped it to find the sharpest, full-length, black leather trench coat

ever. It was the same one she had been raving about to
Jason. She'd spotted it in a Spiegel catalogue, but was
waiting for it to go on sale.

"Oh my," she said in awe. "He's really gone crazy.
Jason . . . ahhhhh . . . ha, ha . . . I love it!" she screamed.

Jason sat on the couch smiling contentedly, soaking
in all of her excitement.

"Come on, Renee, we need to get going," he said,
smiling inside and out.

"Okay, I'm almost dressed," Renee said, finding the
sexiest little red dress she could find. She threw on her
trench and glided down the stairs feeling like a princess.

"Well . . . how do I look?" Renee asked, holding her
hands in the air.

Jason stood in awe of her beauty.

"You look amazing. You're stunning. Absolutely stunning," he said, not able to take his eyes off her. A kiss
snapped him out of his trance.

"Thank you so much for the coat. I love it. I've always
wanted one!"

"I know it. Come on. Let's go," Jason said, taking her
hand.

The drive in the limo was wonderful to say the least.
It was filled with sweet kisses, good conversation, and
soft music. Renee thought this night couldn't get any
better. Where could they be going? she wondered. She
was incredibly caught up in the moment; Jason had a
way of doing that to her. He could be downright evil
one moment, and then the next he was treating her like
royalty. She never considered herself to be materialistic,
but she did love the "finer things in life." When she and
Kay were growing up, Kay was the flamboyant one. She
was the one who had boyfriends showering her with

grand gifts. Renee was the one who stayed home and studied and all she had was great grades to show for it. No teddy bears, jewelry, or school dance invites. Jason worshipped her, though, and she loved it, even if it meant putting up with his bad temper from time to time. It was worth it, especially tonight.

"We're here," Jason said.

"Where? We must have been driving for at least an hour," Renee commented.

"Just a little over an hour," Jason said. "We're up north in the mountains."

"Mountains?" Renee said, surprised. "I can't believe we've been driving that long."

"Time flies when you're having fun, baby," Jason said.

"Wow, it's so beautiful out here. The breeze is so cool. Perfect weather for my new coat . . . tee-hee." Renee chuckled.

They didn't waste any time taking advantage of the luxurious cabin overlooking the mountains. Jasmine-scented candles at every turn and fragrant lilacs filled every room. There were even rose petals scattered on the king-size bed.

"Jason, there's a hot tub out here on the veranda!"

"Nothing is too good for you, baby. I mean that. And this is only the beginning. We have the rest of our lives," Jason said, joining Renee outside.

They lost themselves in the deep, dark sky filled with a million stars. The mountains seemed close enough to reach out and touch. The view was breathtaking and calming. Renee felt a peacefulness that had seemed so foreign for so long. After her night with Kevin she thought it might be over between her and Jason. But she had to let her feelings for Kevin go; he was not an option for her. Blood was much thicker than water, and Kay was too important to her.

"This is the life. I could definitely get used to this," Jason said.

At that moment, he decided to forget about everything that had happened the night of the key party. He wanted to redeem himself, and by the look on Renee's face, he felt like he had done just that. They finished up the night with a skinny-dip in the hot tub. They made love for the first time in weeks. By the time they finished eating and showering, they were both exhausted.

"Come here," Renee said, reaching her hand out to Jason's. "Thank you, Jay, this is exactly what I needed today."

"You're welcome, honey," Jason said as he drifted to sleep.

Renee stroked his hair as he lay with his head in her lap on the couch. They were listening to some soft jazz playing on the radio. She couldn't sleep. She started to think about Kevin again. She couldn't get him out of her mind. *What has he done to me?* she asked herself, frustrated. *How could I be thinking about him after this incredible night I just shared with Jason? What does that mean?* She had to admit to herself that Jason scared her at times with his bipolar characteristics. It was like he was two different people. It scared her even more that she allowed him to treat her like that at all. But she just couldn't help feeling sorry for him when he struggled with his anxiety and depression. She convinced herself that that's what love was about, being there through the good and the bad . . . being supportive. Deep down she knew it was wrong, but she didn't care, she was on such a high tonight; nothing, not even Kevin, was going to bring her down, *as if Kevin ever could*. She chuckled to herself.

She decided that even though she let Jason romance her tonight, she was definitely going to talk to him in the morning. She had to get him to admit what had been going on in his head all these years. She planned on telling him that he couldn't continue to treat her like garbage one day and then shower her with gifts the next. She knew it was her fault for allowing him to do it, but she had to stop. It wasn't right or healthy for either of them. If she was going to marry him, she would have to set him straight. He looked so serene lying in her lap. She figured the least she could do was let him have this night. Renee was on her way to sleep when one of her favorite songs started playing on the radio. It was "Unforgettable," the version with Nat King Cole and his daughter, Natalie.

"Oh, oh . . . Jay, wake up, I love this song," Renee said, jumping up and extending her hand to Jason for a dance.

"Wha . . . what?" Jason said, groggy.

"Get up! This is one of my favorite songs."

When Jason stood up he couldn't move. He was frozen. His eyes stared out into the air as if he had seen a ghost.

"Jay? Are you okay?" Renee asked. But he didn't answer her, he just stood in a trance.

"Jason?" Renee took his face in her hands. "Hey, what's going on? You're scaring me," she said.

Then he blinked, shook his head, and snapped out of it.

"Renee, I'm sorry . . ." Jason said, appearing back to normal. "Come on, baby . . . let's dance . . . I like this song too," and he rose from the couch, pulling Renee into his arms.

"Wow, you're really sweating, Jay, are you sure you're okay? What's going on? Where were you just now?"

"I'm okay, Renee! Let's just dance, the song is almost over."

"I'm sorry, you're right," Renee said, still unsure as she laid her head on Jason's cold, clammy shoulder.

Jason closed his eyes and held Renee tight as they rocked to the music. Nat King Cole's voice flowed through his veins like ice water. He couldn't help but reminisce when hearing the song that had played throughout the house when he would get home from school. He never bought any of his records as an adult and he would always somehow convince Renee not to play them during any of the time they had spent together. He was caught off guard tonight and he wasn't sure how to get it out of his mind, so he lifted Renee's head from his shoulder and began to kiss her. He thought that would make him forget, but it only intensified the madness inside him. Instead of Renee, all he could see was his mother. He began to kiss her hard, his lips pressed against hers with intense passion.

Renee wasn't sure what was going on. It was okay at first. She welcomed his abrasive demeanor; she thought he was maybe getting a little kinky, but then he started to get out of control. He started pulling her hair. He ripped her blouse open, groping and fondling her breasts as if he had been in jail for the last ten years. He broke the clasps on her bra and started to bite on her nipples.

"Ouch!" Renee shrieked as she pushed Jason off her. *"What's wrong with you, what are you doing?"* Renee shrieked.

"Nothing's wrong with me, baby, I'm just giving you what you want."

"Giving me what I want? What are you talking about? You've never touched me like that before. That hurt! What do you think I am . . . some kind of whore off the street that you can treat any kind of way? I don't know what gave you the impression that I would be into that kinda shit, but I'm *not! you better not ever touch me like that again! Do you hear me?*"

"Come on, Renee, I was just trying something new," Jason said, as calm as he could be. "What's wrong? You don't like it when I'm rough? You're being a real bitch," he told her. Then Jason grabbed Renee again. This time he grabbed her throat and started to squeeze her neck, whispering in her ear, "*I know you want it, let me give it to you.*"

"J-a-s-o-n!" Renee screamed, barely able to speak.

"What's the matter? You don't wanna fuck? Is that it?" Jason said, snarling like a maniac.

He started to kiss Renee again. He threw his tongue deep into her mouth. Renee bit his tongue and kneed him in the balls as hard as she could.

"Ahhhhh," Jason yelped, releasing the grip on her throat.

"*Are you out of your fucking mind?*" Renee screamed in sheer horror. Her torn blouse and bra were hanging off her trembling body as she ran toward the telephone.

Jason looked up at her, still holding his bruised privates in his hand. He was beet red and completely enraged. He managed to stumble toward her and yanked the telephone out of her hand and threw it across the room. The telephone smashed into tiny pieces. Renee stood terrified. She couldn't believe what was happening. How had the night gone in this direction? She was utterly confused. The man who was standing in this living room was a Jason that even she hadn't seen before. She was mentally preparing herself to do whatever it took to get out of the room and away from him. He would have to kill her before she would let him touch her again, she thought, looking around the living area for some kind of weapon.

Jason watched as Renee circled the room. "I'm sorry, baby, I don't know what came over me. I didn't know what I was doing. You just caught me off guard waking me up so suddenly," he said, pleading with Renee.

But Renee wasn't buying it.

"Don't start that 'I'm sorry' bullshit, Jason. You called me a bitch. How could you call me that? You're crazy if you think an apology can fix this," Renee told him.

Jason began to cry like a baby. He reached his hand out to Renee for comfort, but found only a cold stare looking back at him. Renee was disgusted. She felt no pity for him, only contempt. She ran into the bedroom, packed her bag, and proceeded to walk out of the cabin, leaving the nightmare behind her.

"Can't we just talk about this?" Jason said. "I need help."

"You squeezed my neck until I couldn't breathe, Jason! Do you understand that? Do you understand that you could have killed me? This is *over!*" she said, walking toward the door and slinging it open.

Jason couldn't do anything but hold his head down as he watched Renee run out of his life. He felt helpless. He knew he had gone too far and he had no idea how to fix it. But he knew one thing; it definitely couldn't be fixed tonight. So, he let her go.

When Renee looked back she saw someone who resembled the Jason she loved. He was in the fetal position crying his eyes out. It didn't make her feel sorry enough to want to go back. She kept her composure as she walked about a half mile up to the front office. The old man at the front desk looked puzzled when he saw Renee sobbing with her bag in hand.

"I need a cab immediately," she said, wiping the tears from her eyes.

"A cab? At this hour? Where you headed, ma'am, didn't you just check in?"

"I'm going back to Atlanta."

"It's a pretty long way to Atlanta in a cab . . . you sure you wanna go?"

"*Yes*, just call them please. I'm sure!" Renee walked out of the front office and sat on the porch. She was devastated. She wanted to know what was going on with Jason. She wanted to go back and ask him what the hell happened, but she couldn't. She was terrified. She just wanted to go home and sleep in her own bed. The cab took about thirty minutes, but once it arrived, Renee had calmed down considerably.

"Where to?" the cabdriver asked.

"Atlanta," Renee said as she lay back. She started to cry again. She felt like she was in the twilight zone. She wrapped herself in the leather trench Jason gave her. But she still felt cold.

The next morning Renee buried herself in work. Her coworkers all asked what happened to her voice. She was extremely hoarse from Jason squeezing her throat. She just told them she must be coming down with something. She wore a scarf to cover up the marks on her neck, but there was nothing she could wear to cover up what had happened to her, no matter how much she wanted to.

Fifteen

Kevin and Kay

Kay was on top of the world when she left the gym after work early Wednesday afternoon. She had finally gotten up the nerve to call Brian and see what he had to say. He told her that he felt very strongly that the fact they met had not been a coincidence and thought they should explore the possibility of going into the real estate business together. Kay had never thought of starting her own business, but it made perfect sense. He just told her to think about it and see if it was something she might be interested in. He was extremely business-savvy and Kay had great experience to go along with that. She was getting excited just thinking about the possibility. She told him she would give him a call later in the week and that they could do lunch to discuss it further.

She couldn't wait to tell Kevin about it. He would be supportive, no doubt. She loved that about him. She was convinced that Kevin was the right man for her. Cool, cute, funny, and smart. She didn't need anything else to make her happy. Besides, she always felt that

Kevin loved her wild side. And she was glad because that would never change. This was one of the things that she scored major points with Kevin on since Renee was so quiet. She knew that there had always been some chemistry between him and Renee, but she believed that the reason it never went any further was that he loved how crazy she was. In the end, Renee would only bore him. That was one of the reasons she agreed to the key party knowing there was a chance he might pick Renee's key. She secretly wanted him to pick Renee so that he could see her for the nerd she really was. "Ha, ha," she laughed to herself. She figured Renee would turn him off once he got to spend some real time with her.

She was drenched with sweat from head to toe and full of energy. She couldn't wait to share the news with Kevin. She rushed home and took a quick shower and decided to call him at work. She only got his voice mail, so she left him a message. "Hey, baby, I can't believe you're not there. I'm on cloud nine and need you here to float with me. Can you come over tonight? Call me, okay? Love you."

Kay was so disappointed that she didn't get Kevin, but she knew he would come over once he got her message. She had noticed that he had been somewhat distant lately. Ever since the key party, they hadn't made love or even talked about it. She tried to get him to talk about the party once on Sunday, but he just used the "we're not supposed to discuss what happened" line, so she left it alone. Deep down, she wondered what happened and whom he'd picked. She decided to call Renee to see what she was up to and to try and squeeze some info out of her. Knowing Renee, though, she would probably stick like glue to the promise she'd made not to talk about the party.

When Renee answered the phone, Kay immediately knew something was wrong.

"Are you okay, Renee? You sound funny," Kay said, concerned.

"Yeah, I'm okay. Just sitting here relaxing. I saw Jason last night and as usual we had a huge fight. To be honest, we broke up."

"What! Why, what happened?" Kay asked.

"Nothing, I don't really want to talk about it, Kay, I just want to forget it for right now. I'm sure I'll be ready to fill you in tomorrow or something when I'm not so emotional and it's not so fresh in my mind."

"Are you sure?" Kay asked. "I could come over if you want. I want to help."

"Yeah, I'm sure. Thanks for the concern, though, I'll be okay. I just need some time to myself," Renee told Kay.

"Well, okay, if you need to talk, let me know, I'm always here for you."

"I will, Kay, thanks, bye."

Kay decided not to tell Renee her good news or grill her for details on the party. She thought it would be inappropriate under the circumstances. Kay hung up the phone, feeling helpless. She wondered what could have happened to make Jason and Renee actually break things off completely. She couldn't help but wonder if it had to do with Kevin. How coincidental for her and Jason to break up so soon after the party. She was more curious than ever to find out if Kevin pulled Renee's key. Could that be why Kevin had been so distant? She had to know. She wondered if Jason would give up some info on things.

Her fingers were dialing Jason's number against her better judgment. When she heard his voice on the other end, she knew she had made a mistake.

"Hello," Jason answered for the second time.

"Hey, Jason, it's Kay."

"Kay? Did Renee tell you to call me?"

"Nooooooo, Jason. No, she didn't." Kay thought it was best not to mention the conversation that she and Renee had had about things being over. Besides, she wanted Jason to be on her side for the moment.

"So what's up then?" Jason said.

"Well, ummmm, hmmmmmm, how do I say this?"

"Just say it, Kay, what's up?" Jason was sure she was calling about him and Renee. Why else would she be calling him?

"Okay, I'm just going to spit it out. Do you know who picked Renee on the night of the key party?"

There was dead silence on the other end of the phone.

"Jason? Hello? Are you there?"

"Yeah, I'm here. You know we're not supposed to talk about any of this, Kay."

"Come on, Jason, I just need to know. I have my reasons. It's more than just curiosity, trust me."

"Since you asked, Kay, I'll tell you. I mean, why should I be the only one to suffer in this nightmare? Kevin picked Renee's key."

Kay didn't say a word; she was shocked. She didn't expect Jason to tell her. Her mind was going a million miles per hour.

"Come on, Kay . . . don't get all quiet on me. I mean, we both know what's up with those two," Jason said in a righteous tone. He wanted to blame everything on Kevin. But deep down he knew that Renee's breaking it off with him had nothing to do with Kevin. He had to fix himself, and until he did, he wasn't going to ever make anyone happy, himself included.

"So you're saying that you know for a fact that Kevin picked Renee's key?" Kay asked.

"Yup," Jason told her. "I know because I was there that night. I saw them together."

"What do you mean you saw them together?" Kay started asking questions she didn't want the answers to, but she was too far gone now. Her curiosity was killing her. She felt sick inside. The last few days were all starting to come together now. Kevin's distance, him not wanting to make love, Renee and Jason breaking up. *I mean, Kevin hasn't cracked one single joke since the night of the key party*, she thought to herself. It was like her biggest nightmare unfolding right before her very eyes.

"I bet you wish you hadn't called me . . . huh?" Jason said, egging Kay on.

"I'm sorry I bothered you, Jay, I have to go."

"No problem, Kay, let me know if you need anything else," Jason said, proud of what he had done. He hung up the phone feeling a little sorry for her, but he enjoyed sticking it to Kevin. He was so filled with jealousy and rage he couldn't make a right move at this point. He wasn't thinking clearly anymore. He had convinced himself that he was nothing without Renee. It had taken him so long to love a woman . . . to make love to a woman. Renee was essentially the love of his life and now she was gone. He knew that she would never take him back now. Renee was a forgiving woman, but she would never be able to forgive what he did last night. He couldn't even forgive himself. He wanted so badly to forget about his mother. He wanted to forget she ever existed. He just wanted the pain to go away. He decided to call Chris and ask him to come over. He was the one person he felt he could trust and he wanted to come clean about it all. He didn't know why, but he just had to do it.

Chris got to Jason's place about thirty minutes later. When he got there he had no idea what to expect. Jason told him everything; he told him about his mother and his father. He told him that he had sex repeatedly with her and that it broke something inside him that could never be fixed. Chris asked him why he never went into therapy. Jason hated the thought of "shrinks." He felt that most of them had the same problems as their patients. Besides, he couldn't have imagined doing what he had just done. He had intended to take this dirty secret to the grave. He was disgusted with himself. He felt dirty and forever tainted. Chris felt terrible. He didn't know what to do for his friend. It all made so much sense to Chris, the rage, the outbreaks, the insecurity. He told Jason that he would be there for him to help him get through it. That together they would find a way to fight the demons and that the first step was to tell Renee.

"*No*," Jason said, in tears. "Renee can never know what happened."

"Jason, you have to tell her. Renee is such a beautiful person. She will be there for you. I know she would give you the support you need, the love that you deserve, the love you never received as a child. She already loves you so much."

"Not anymore. She hates me. You don't know what I did to her last night," Jason said, crying uncontrollably.

"What did you do? What happened?"

"I—I practically raped her . . . I was violent with her.

I even put my hands around her throat. I could have killed her, Chris. I was out of control."

"You did what?" Chris said in shock. He knew that Jason had a lot of anger in him, but he never thought he would take it that far.

"Listen, Jason, you have to get help and you have got to tell Renee what the root to all of your problems has been."

"No, Chris, you have to promise me . . . promise me that you will never tell anyone what I've told you. Not even Nikki. I couldn't stand for them to all look at me that way."

"What way?"

"Like a victim . . . with pity in their eyes . . . the way you're looking at me right now."

"I don't pity you, Jason, I pity your mother. You have to realize that she was sick too. She didn't know what she was doing. She wasn't the monster. You were both victims. And until you come to terms with that you will never be able to move on. You have to forgive her, and even more importantly, you have to forgive yourself."

"You're a good friend, Chris. That's why I called you. But I'm tired, maan. I'm real tired. I will think about what you said. I just want to go to sleep now. My head will be much clearer in the morning."

"All right, I'll let you get some rest. But think about what I said, okay?"

"I will, man, I will. Hey, what about that card game?" Jason said, smiling and wiping his face.

"Oh . . . oh . . . yeah, I'll let you know tomorrow," Chris told him. "Me and Rick are gonna be playing some ball later on today, so I'll see what his schedule is like."

"Cool, hey, tell Rick I said 'what's up?' "

"I will. I'll hit you back tomorrow."

"Later."

Chris drove home angry at the world. He felt utterly helpless and alone with this huge weight on his shoulders. How could he go on without telling anybody what had happened to Jason? How would he keep quiet the next time Nikki started dogging Jason about how bad he treated Renee? But he made a promise to his friend that he was going to keep. One that he would take to his grave. Besides, he figured he would just try and convince Jason to come clean and go get some help. At least he hoped.

Later that evening Kay sat at home pissed off at the information she had gotten from Jason. She couldn't believe that her worst fear had come true. Her sister and Kevin had been together in ways that she couldn't even begin to think of. No wonder the muthafucker was avoiding her. And of course, Renee would be distraught over all of this. Kay wanted to throw up. Actually she wanted to throw a brick through Kevin's truck window. She had to get her mind right; she really had no cause to be upset with either of them, but she couldn't help it. What could she do? She agreed to the key party, knowing that this could happen. She played Kevin picking Renee's key a million times in her head, but now it was no longer a game. Kevin had sex with her sister. She wasn't going to be able to think straight until she talked to Kevin. She figured the best thing to do was to continue playing her role as if she didn't know a thing. That's the only way Kevin was going to talk to her about anything. She was so happy about the great things going on in her life she thought she would try and focus on that.

She put on some Eric Benet and her favorite pair of sweats and attempted to put herself out of the misery she was in until Kevin arrived. She had thought about whipping up a quick meal but decided to order a pizza instead. She poured a glass of wine and fell back on the couch to relax. She knew Kevin could use his own key to get into her place, so she let herself drift off to sleep. She awoke to the sound of a loud bang on her front door. She looked out the peephole and saw the pizza guy staring her back in the face.

After she paid the deliveryman and took the pizza into the kitchen she realized she had been sleep for a while. It was 11:00 p.m. and Kevin still hadn't shown up. She couldn't believe it. He always came over to check up on her whether he returned her call or not. She took for granted that today wouldn't be any different, but it was. He didn't call her and he didn't come over. She called him at home and got no answer. She decided against leaving another desperate message. She hung up and began crying. Where the hell was he? At this point, she was even worried that he might have been in an accident. She decided to go through the dreaded chore of calling around to hospitals to see if there was any record of him coming through their ER. She came up with nothing again. Now she was really mad. Could he be with Renee? Having just spoken to Renee earlier that evening, she didn't pick up on anything in her voice that would tell Kay that Renee was lying. She called every one of their friends. Chris said that Kevin had dropped by the courts around nine and shot a few hoops and then broke out, not mentioning where he was going, though. Now she had no doubt he was avoiding her. What the fuck was going on!

Renee had just gotten out of the shower when she heard the doorbell ringing relentlessly. It was late so she couldn't imagine who it could be, hoping it wasn't Jason. As she threw on her thick white terry cloth robe, she noticed the marks on her neck, and the bite marks on her shoulder. *If that's Jason I'm going to freak. He couldn't have the audacity to show up here after what he's done,* she thought to herself as she headed down the stairs toward the front door. When she looked through the peephole she was surprised to see Kevin. She dimmed the lights in the living room so he wouldn't see the dark marks on her neck. Opening the door, she saw his beautiful body glistening with sweat. He was panting like he had just run a marathon.

"Kevin? What are you doing here?"

"Can I come in?" he asked.

"Of course, let me get you a towel. Where have you been and why are you so wet?"

"Well, I was playing basketball with Rick and Chris and then I ran over here."

"You ran all the way over here? Kevin, that's not possible. Do you know how far that is?"

"Ah, yeah, I think I do. Can't be more than a mile," and they both started to laugh. His bright white teeth sparkled through the dim light in her living room.

"I'm not going to sit . . . you know, being all sweaty and all . . . unless you want me to take another shower?" Kevin said with a devilish grin.

"Ha, ha . . . you're funny. No, I think I'll keep you away from that shower tonight, okay?"

"I'm just playing, Renee . . . seriously, though, I needed to see you."

"What's up?" Her heart felt like it was going to pound right out of her chest. Only Kevin could make her heart pound like that. She couldn't stand that. She hoped he couldn't notice how nervous she was.

"Do I make you nervous?" Kevin asked.

"Nah, why do you ask?" she said, feeling faint.

"I don't know, you just fidget a lot when I'm around you. I guess that's just something you do, then."

"Whatever, I'm not fidgeting. I'm just tired, I guess. What's up? What are you doing here?"

"Well, two reasons. First, I wanted to ask you how your presentation went yesterday."

"You didn't run all the way over here to ask me that," Renee said, looking suspicious.

"Didn't I say I had two reasons? Now answer the question. How did it go?"

"*It went great, Kevin,*" Renee said in a sarcastic tone.

"Goooood. I'm so glad it worked out. So do you think you guys are going to get the account?"

"Kevin, what the hell are you doing here? I mean, I get that you're happy for me . . . but you obviously have something pretty important on your mind. I mean, look at you. Kay said that you have been acting a little strange. What's going on?"

"Well, to tell you the truth, I haven't been able to get you out of my mind. I mean, I've really tried, Renee, but I just can't stop thinking about our night together."

Renee took a deep breath and sat down. She was floored at Kevin's confession. She hadn't expected him to be so honest. She had felt the same way, but thought she would never let him know. It was easier for her to chalk it up to the game and pretend it didn't really mean anything, but she knew that it did. She knew that night was special and she was glad that Kevin had been the one to say it instead of her.

"Renee? Did you hear what I said?"

"Yes, I'm sorry, Kevin, I'm so sleepy, can we talk about this another time?" she said, wanting him to leave. She wasn't ready to face any of it. Not her feelings for Kevin, not her shambles of a relationship or engagement, for that matter, with Jason, none of it.

"No, we can't talk about this another time. Do you know that I haven't spoken to Kay in days? I didn't go to work, I haven't checked my messages at home or on my cell phone. All in an attempt to avoid her and her questions. I can't do it anymore!" Kevin raised his voice slightly. "She knows something's up and I can't lie to her anymore."

"What are you saying?" Renee gasped. "Are you going to tell Kay what happened?"

"That's why I'm here. I wanna know what you think happened that night, Renee."

"Nothing happened. I mean, nothing that wasn't supposed to happen. I mean, it was a game. We were drunk and got caught up, that's all," Renee said, lying her ass off.

"Renee," Kevin said, walking closer to her.

He was standing so close she could feel the heat generating from his body. She looked up into his brown eyes. She wanted to dive right in. She wanted to admit her feelings to him too. But she was too afraid. What would this mean for her and Kay? Kay loved him so much. Renee couldn't take that away from her. And then there was Jason, of course. Even though she told him it was over, she still loved him. She still had to come to terms with her feelings for him and realize that he wasn't the man she needed to be marrying. She wasn't emotionally ready to handle the feelings she had for Kevin. So, she did the cowardly thing and lied.

"Kevin, don't. I can't do this right now."

"Do what? Feel? Kiss me? Kiss me without there being a game between us?"

"Kevin, the night of the key party was special for me too. I wanted to make love to you. But I believe we didn't make love for a reason. It wasn't meant to be. My sister is obviously in love with you. It's all just way too complicated and there's too much at stake here. We can't be together. We just can't."

Kevin's initial response was to fight for what he wanted. To argue to no end with Renee about how she felt. But he knew she was right.

"I'm sorry I came here, Renee, I . . . I just needed to get some clarity, you know . . . I . . . I'll leave now," Kevin said, backing off. He was hurt. Hurt more deeply than he'd ever been. Kay was in love with him and he loved Kay too. There were too many factors involved that just weren't in their favor. It was just bad timing. As he started to walk out the door, he stopped dead in his tracks and turned around.

"Renee, will you do one thing for me?" Kevin asked, walking toward her now.

"Yeah, Kevin," she said, looking down, trying to hold back tears.

"Let me kiss you just one more time. I've wanted to kiss you again ever since that time in the closet. It's the only way I can walk away from you right now. Please don't deny me one last kiss," he pleaded.

Renee stood silent, gazing into Kevin's eyes. She wanted to kiss him too. She had imagined kissing Kevin so many times it was crazy. Her knees buckled as he slowly made his way toward her. They were lost in each other's eyes. His hand gently reached up and caressed her face. Renee's eyes closed and a tear slid down her cheek. She turned her face to the left slightly and kissed his hand softly. Kevin's desire for her was almost uncontrollable at that point. He wanted to take his request back. If he kissed her now, he would want her forever. He went with his heart, and their lips met for the first time in over a year. Kevin's lips were tender and soft, Renee's luscious and sweet. They wanted to live in each other's arms for an eternity. Renee put her arms around Kevin's neck and pulled him closer to her. When Kevin felt Renee's body against his he knew he had to stop or it would go on forever. He let her face go and took a step back. He stared at her and was at a loss for words. They gave each other a look that assuredly said they were doing the right thing. They couldn't cross the line any further or they would never make it back to the other side.

"Please don't be mad at me, Kevin," Renee said, stepping away.

"I could never be mad at you, Renee. I love you." They were both surprised by his words but he continued talking. "I understand why we can't be together, but I want you to know something, and it's something you may not like. I can't be with Kay, I just can't. She deserves much better than this. I won't tell her about my feelings for you, but I can't stay with her knowing I love you."

"Kevin, you can't break up with her. It would absolutely kill her," Renee told him, sounding desperate.

"And don't think she's naïve. She'll know exactly why you're doing it. How long do you think it will take her to figure this out if she hasn't already? She will immediately try to find out if your breaking up with her has something to do with the party. Especially since me and Jason are over!"

"What?" Kevin said, surprised.

"Ugh," Renee said under her breath. She didn't mean to blurt that out.

"What do you mean you and Jason are through? What happened?"

"Nothing, Kevin. I don't want to talk about it."

"No, Renee, we're going to talk about it. What's going on? What did he do to you that night?"

"Nothing. He passed out. That's it. End of story. You gotta go now, Kevin," Renee said, grabbing Kevin's arm and leading him toward the door.

Kevin turned on the living room light. He wanted to see Renee's face. He knew she was hiding something from him. That's when he noticed her neck.

"What the hell happened to your neck?" He tilted her head up to the light and saw the dark circles around her throat.

"What's going on, Renee? Talk to me. Did he do this?" Kevin said, raising his voice.

"*No!*" Renee screamed. "Kevin, just go, I can't do this right now."

"Either you tell me or I'll go find out from Jason. Now which way do you want it to go?"

"It was an accident. I swear. He didn't mean for it to happen."

"Not good enough. How the hell did he accidentally put his hands around your throat so hard that he bruised you?"

"Kevin . . . please go."

"I'll go all right . . . I'm going straight to Jason's. That muthafucka thinks he is so crazy. I'm gonna show him crazy. I'm going to beat the shit out of him. An ass whuppin' is the best thing for crazy."

"Noooooooooo, Kevin," Renee begged. "Please don't do that. Look, I told him that it's over, and he left. Please don't rile him up again. You'll only make things worse."

But Kevin wasn't listening to Renee. He ran out the door so fast she couldn't even catch him.

"*Keeeeevin,*" Renee screamed. But it was too late. He was gone.

Kevin ran all the way back to the gym. He got in his car and drove straight to Jason's. He couldn't believe what this fool had done. Jason was a bigger asshole than Kevin had thought he was. Kevin was thinking of all the ways he was going to kick Jason's ass. "He's never, ever gonna touch her again," Kevin said out loud to himself. The entire way there all he did was get hyped up. He and Jason had never been tight by any means. But Kevin never thought the day would come when he would be smiling at the thought of beating Jason beyond recognition. There had always been a little tension since the night they played spin the bottle, but that was so long ago. He and Jason had hung out a few times, just the two of them, and they always had a good time. For the most part, Kevin just thought Jason was a little strange at times. Real high-strung. Real emotional. But Kevin would just make a joke of it and then they would be cool again. He couldn't believe that Renee was trying to protect him at this point. He could see

Jason's house by now and saw Jason's car in the driveway.

He rang the bell several times and got no answer. He started to bang on the door mercilessly.

"*Jason, you better answer this door or I'm gonna bust this shit down,*" Kevin yelled.

The door opened immediately and Jason stood there with pillow marks on his face.

"What the fuck do you want, Kevin, are you trying to wake all of my neighbors up?" Jason said, half asleep.

Kevin didn't give him a chance to say another word. He jumped Jason, tackling him to the floor, and started wailing on him all over. He was punching him in the face, ribs, and chest all at the same time, it seemed to Jason. Jason didn't fight back at first, but once he realized he was getting his ass lit up he found the strength to kick Kevin off him.

"What the hell is your problem?" Jason snapped, totally confused. He was barely able to catch the blood that had started pouring from his mouth.

"I'll tell you what the problem is. Those marks you left on Renee's throat, that's what the problem is."

"What does that have to do you with you?" Jason said, cocky as hell. "You've been to see her already, huh? You couldn't wait a week for us to be broken up before you took your black ass over to her, huh?" he said in disgust.

"You know what, man, I don't have to explain shit to you," Kevin told him, waving his hand in Jason's face. "What the fuck did you do to her?" he said, rushing Jason again. Jason ducked just in time, sending Kevin's hand crashing into the wall. It left a huge hole and Kevin knew he had to have broken it.

"Damn it!" Kevin yelled, grabbing his hand. It was cut and started to bleed.

"That's what you get," Jason said, looking at Kevin's hand, with a bloody grin on his face.

"Don't worry about me," Kevin told Jason. "You need to worry about why your woman has more love for me than she ever had for you. And be thankful that I decided to let her go."

"Ohhhhhhh, so you think you've got Renee, do you? Is that what you think? Nigga, please. Renee will be back. Believe that, and there ain't shit you can do about it."

"How could you put your hands on her like that?"

"Me and Renee's affairs are none of your business, now get the fuck out."

"Yeah, well, we'll see about that. You just watch your back, and stay away from her, you got that?"

"I don't gotta do shit. We'll see who has Renee in the end. You may get her for a second. But trust me. That's all you'll get, a second! She'll forgive me. Believe that! And when she does, I'll be right here waiting for her. So go ahead and go home to her look-alike. She may even be a better fuck!"

Just for the hell of it Kevin turned around and body-slammed Jason one more time and spat in his face as he rose to his feet.

"That was for the shit you said about Kay. Keep it up, Jason, and you're gonna end up in a real bad situation," Kevin told him on his way out. He got up and walked out of Jason's house. When he got into his truck he realized he was hurting a little too. His hand was the only visible sign that he had been in a fight. It hit that wall pretty hard. It had already started swelling, but he figured he would nurse it some himself tonight before going to a doctor to have it checked out. He spent the drive home thinking about how crazy life had gotten for all of them. It wasn't because of any one thing, he guessed. The key party had simply uncovered underlying issues that had always been there.

He pulled up to his house and smiled at the fact that he was finally home. When he finally got inside he almost jumped out of his skin when he noticed the silhouette sitting on his couch. It was Kay. All he could think when he saw her was how she couldn't have picked a worse time to surprise him.

"Long time no see," Kay said, looking pissed.

"Hey, Kay," Kevin said, tucking his hands in his pockets.

"Where have you been?"

"Long story, Kay, and I really don't want to get into it right now. I'm just gonna take a quick shower and go to bed. Can we talk about all of this tomorrow?"

"*Hell no*, we can't talk about this shit tomorrow. Now what's going on, Kevin? I think I deserve a fucking explanation."

"I know you do, Kay, and you'll get one, trust me, just not tonight. Can't you see I'm beat?"

"Beat from what?"

Kevin realized that he was going to have to tell Kay something. He knew how stubborn she was.

"I've had a long couple of days," Kevin told her. "Starting with things not working out with two of my players that were caught cheating."

"Listen, Kevin, I don't give a damn about that right now. Where have you been and why have you been avoiding me? I've left messages for you at work, at home, with Chris and Rick."

"I got a couple of them," Kevin said. "And I called you," he told her, telling the first of many lies to get himself out of the mess he had created.

"And you didn't think to leave any messages?" Kay said, continuing to grill Kevin.

"Well, that's just it . . . I knew I needed to talk to you and I tried to call you and didn't get an answer. That's when I decided to call you at Renee's to see if you might be over there. When I spoke to Renee she said you weren't there, but there was something weird in her voice. She sounded really bad. So I thought I would check it out on my way home."

"Yeah, I spoke to her today, too. She and Jason broke up, that's why she probably sounded like that," Kay said, jumping in.

"Yeah, I found that out and a lot more than I bargained for," Kevin told Kay. "He put his hands on her."

"What do you mean?" Kay asked, getting visibly upset.

"Her neck was all marked up from where he had obviously choked her or something. When I asked her what happened she didn't want to talk about it, so I left and headed straight to Jason's."

"You went to Jason's? Why?"

"To confront him, that's why."

"Well, what did he say?"

"He didn't say anything. He said it was none of my business. We went back and forth for a while and then I left."

"Well, I wish you would have left a message or something when you tried to call me. I was pretty disappointed when you didn't show up at my place tonight," Kay said, unsatisfied with Kevin's excuse for standing her up.

"I know, I'm sorry. I was in such a funk today. I wasn't doing anything right."

"I even called hospitals looking for you. I guess I

should be glad you're all right," Kay said, grabbing Kevin's hand.

"Ouch!"

"Oh my God! Look at your hand!"

"It's cool, baby."

"How did that happen? Did you and Jason fight?"

"No . . . well, yeah, a little. I took a swing and missed and hit the wall. It's not a big deal."

"It was that deep, Kevin?"

"Deep? He physically abused your sister. What are you talking about? Hell yeah, I busted his ass."

Silence filled the room as Kay gazed in his eyes. At that moment she realized the depth of Kevin's feelings for Renee. And it killed her. She wanted to know what he had really been doing at Renee's. She wanted to tell him that she knew about how he really felt about her sister, but she couldn't. If he knew that she called Jason to spy on him he would be so pissed. She decided to keep that bit of information to herself for now.

"Wow. Well, I guess I should thank you for coming to my sister's rescue."

"Well, I had to . . . I mean, what would you have thought of me if I didn't go over there in her defense?" Kevin said, knowing he was full of shit.

"I'm gonna take a shower and head to bed . . . you coming?" he said, reaching his hand out to Kay.

"Sure," Kay said, feeling as if she were a million miles away. She decided to wait and tell Kevin her good news another time. Her spirit was broken.

That night they lay together, but they were further apart than they'd ever been. Kay lay awake asking herself how she could continue to stay in a relationship with a man who was in love with her sister. She knew Kevin loved her but not the way he loved Renee. She wanted to be strong and just tell him to go to hell. But she couldn't. She loved him and needed him. Instead, she thought she would try to make him forget about Renee. She didn't know how she was going to do it, but she would find a way.

Kevin awoke in the middle of the night and went into the kitchen. He took an ice-cold beer out of the fridge and downed it in one swig. He thought about how much lying he had done tonight. It wasn't something he was proud of, but the truth would have hurt her more and he didn't want that. He couldn't help but think of Renee; kissing her, touching her, holding her in his arms. That last kiss had confirmed their true feelings for each other. He wondered if he could ever grow to love Kay the way he loved Renee. He knew he had to try. Renee was not an option anymore.

Sixteen

Rick and Lynda

Lynda had never had a harder time in life than when she pulled out a suitcase and started to pack her things. Her friends had been so supportive of her decision, so that made things a lot easier. But looking around her bedroom now, "their" bedroom, she felt all the memories come rushing back to mind. She had loved Rick all her adult life, for the most part. He had always been there, and for the longest time she thought he always would. But she decided that true love meant letting people go in some cases. Allowing them to find their true destiny and to reach their full potential in life and in love. And that's what she wanted for herself and for Rick. She couldn't believe that nearly a week had passed since the party. Rick suspected that something was wrong with her and had even asked if everything was okay in the last couple of days. He had seemed kind of standoffish to her as well. She figured he knew that she just needed some space for whatever reason, so he was giving it to her. She appreciated it too. He had stayed out pretty late the last couple of nights and they hadn't talked much. She decided that he had picked up on the vibe and knew that something had gone terribly wrong. He was having a hard time dealing with it already, Lynda thought to herself. And that was the hardest part about all of this. Letting Rick down easy was all she thought about. What would be the easiest way to tell him or what was the fairest thing to say? She had to tell him about her true feelings. That she loved women and that he would never be able to satiate this desire that lived inside her.

She had two small suitcases packed already and hidden in the very back of her closet. This was not going to be one of those made-for-TV movie breakups with screaming and yelling. They didn't hate each other and she refused to let it go down that way. Not after all these years. She had even decided to let him keep the house. She was going to move to California, more than likely. She had a couple of contacts and several of her present clients lived on both coasts. Lynda figured it would be easy to start her business over in California. Everyone there wanted to exercise, eat right, and look good. She would just have to figure out a way to make what she had to offer different from what all the other personal trainers were doing out there. Nikki and the girls had offered to make the drive with her out there and just fly themselves back. It would be much cheaper than for her to have to ship her car out there. And right now she needed to save money as much as possible. She would ask Rick to split their savings down the middle and that would be it. She would have her car to take and about twenty-five thousand in cash to start her entire life over. That was more than a lot of people had, though, she figured. She could do it.

She had asked Rick to meet her at a neutral place that didn't hold any memories for the both of them. The Waffle Palace on North Avenue. Not the most up-scale place, but hell, this wasn't *Dynasty*. He had agreed and said it was perfect timing and that he needed to talk to her as well. They had agreed on 7:00 p.m. She figured that if they made a scene they would just quietly pay their tab and leave and finish the conversation in the car. She decided to go ahead and get going so he wouldn't have to wait anxiously for her too long.

Her stomach did flips the entire drive toward down-town. She got sick once on the way and had to actually pull off the road and throw up. It amazed her how love could get you so mixed up inside. She was scared at this point. Scared of what Rick would say, what he would do, how he would react. She knew he wasn't crazy enough to jump off a bridge or anything even close. And for the most part she knew he wouldn't get violent in any way. It was just too much to think about and she wanted to be there now, so she could just see his face and get it over with.

When she pulled up and parked she saw that Rick was already there. He was always on time, Lynda thought to herself, smiling. She was thankful for that. He was sit-ting there all alone and had ordered something for both of them to munch on.

"Hey, babe," she said, walking over and kissing his forehead.

"Hey, Lynda." He looked like he had been crying or maybe just drinking heavily.

"So what's the deal?" Rick said, looking Lynda di-rectly in the eyes. It seemed as if he could already see the words that were about to come out of her mouth.

"Rick, what I'm about to say isn't what you want to

hear," Lynda said, looking down at the waffle sitting in front of her. "But it's something I have to say regardless. It's what's best for both of us in the long run . . . I'm leaving."

She couldn't look up at that point. Her neck felt too heavy to even lift her head up and she didn't want to see Rick's face. When she did finally look up Rick wasn't even looking at her. He was looking toward the door that had just opened. A tall black guy walked in and was looking around. Rick waved at him and the guy began walking their way. Lynda figured it was one of Rick's business partners. They always saw someone he knew whenever they were out. He came over and stood at their booth. Lynda waited to be introduced, as always.

"Lynda, this is T.J. T.J., this is my wife, Lynda."

"Nice to meet you," Lynda said, giving Rick a look as if to say, "Get him out of here, we're busy, don't you think."

"Have a seat," Rick said and T.J. took the space beside Rick.

"I'm sorry," Lynda said out loud, "but, Rick, could we do this another time? I'd really like to finish things up here first."

"I understand, honey, but it's important that he stays for this too."

"What?" Lynda said, completely confused.

"Lynda, T.J. and I have been seeing each other regularly for the past six months. We're lovers."

Lynda's life all came crashing down on her at once. Everything started to make sense at that moment as she started reflecting on things. She kept looking at the both of them. She looked as if she were watching a tennis match the way her head kept moving back and forth looking at Rick and then T.J.

"He's your lover! You have got to be fucking kidding me. Are you kidding me? This is no time for jokes, Rick."

"Why would I even begin to joke about something like this?" Rick said. "Do you think this is easy for me, Lynda? Do you think it was easy for me to admit to myself that I'm in love with a man? Or that I love this man in a way that I never loved you? Huh, Lynda?"

They were getting loud now and the little hillbilly family seated across from them was looking on as they chewed their hash browns and steak.

"No, I don't think it was easy. Why the fuck did he have to be here for you to tell me this bullshit, though?" Lynda said, gesturing toward T.J.

"Lynda," T.J. said, "he was too scared to—"

"*I wasn't talking to you,*" Lynda said loudly.

"You don't have to yell," T.J. said.

"I *SAID* I wasn't talking to you," Lynda said again. "Where did you two meet?" she asked Rick.

Rick had already decided against admitting meeting T.J. through the escort service. Instead he just said they met at the gym a while back and became workout partners.

"It eventually progressed to what it is now," Rick said.

"And what is it? What do you call this? Are you telling me that you are *gay?*" Lynda asked, looking utterly shocked.

"Love," Rick said. "I call this true love. I don't expect you to like it or even to understand it, Lynda, but just respect me and my decision. This doesn't have to get ugly."

"I'll do more than that," Lynda said. "I'm out of here. I cannot believe my fucking eyes or ears. At least you had the decency to tell me yourself. I guess it doesn't matter why I was leaving you since you were already leaving me," she said, thinking of how ironic it all was.

"Hold up . . . you were leaving me? Is that why you called me here?" Rick said, finally paying attention to Lynda.

"Well, if you weren't so busy looking for your boyfriend, you would have heard me tell you that I'm leaving you. I'll be out of the house by this evening. I want half of our savings and that's it. I'll keep my car, you can keep yours, and you can even have the house. If you decide to sell the house later, we'll split that in half too. I don't want anything else. I just want out," Lynda said.

"That all sounds fair to me," Rick said, hurt that she had obviously given this a lot of thought.

T.J. had learned his lesson and was keeping quiet.

"I'll see you at the house later tonight to finalize everything. Very nice to meet you," Lynda said to T.J. The sarcasm in her statement was thick.

She walked out of the Waffle Palace and was able to hold it all together, at least until she got into the parking lot. She couldn't believe it. She was so concerned about Rick all this time while he had been planning to leave her for T.J. How did this happen? When did this happen? How could she have missed the signs? She started to laugh hysterically. She and her husband were both gay. She got into the car and fought the urge to throw up again. Instead, she turned her music up as loud as it would go. She put her shades on and drove home for the very last time.

Seventeen

Cali

Lynda pulled into her driveway and realized that the house already seemed foreign. Or, maybe it had never really felt like home. She called Nikki quickly and told her what had happened. She didn't feel like going into detail. She asked if Nikki could leave as early as tomorrow to drive to Cali with her. Nikki said she would and that she would call Kay and Renee to tell them to get their shit packed too. Lynda thanked Nikki and hung up. She spent the rest of the night packing. Her clothes and shoes were the easiest to pack. When it got down to all the little things, the sentimental things that Rick had given her over the years, that's when she lost it. She started crying and talking to herself out loud, angry at herself and at Rick as well. But she knew inside it wasn't anybody's fault. They had both given it the old college try to make the marriage work. But it had been doomed from the beginning. And that's the thing about life and marriages in general. People will change and all you can hope is that the changes aren't so extreme that they

destroy the foundations that have taken years to build.
She had so many questions. Was Rick always gay? Did
she ever satisfy him sexually? She was in such denial
over the years about her sexuality that she could honestly say that she and Rick had had a lot of good times
in the bedroom. She had loved him practically all of her
life. The passion was real for a long time because of
that. Lynda finished her drink and made another while
she listened to Sade softly. She would miss Rick terribly.
More than anything they had grown to be great friends
who shared a lot of the same interests.

She made sure she packed away all of her address
books that had her clients' contact information in it.
She would have to call all of them when she got to Cali
and tell them she had relocated. It wasn't the most pro-
fessional way to do things, but sometimes you could
only do things the best way you could do them. Rick
would have to handle telling his family what happened,
and this was one time Lynda didn't mind not having
much family. She called U-Haul and scheduled a pickup
for one of their smallest hitches early in the morning.
She would have everything packed and ready to load
waiting by the door.

After she finished packing, she realized she couldn't
spend another night there. Not amidst all the things
that she and Rick had shared. She called the U-Haul
place back and told them she would be there in twenty
minutes to pick up the hitch. She was crying now, uncontrollably. She threw on a hat and grabbed her purse.
She had left a message for Nikki telling her not to worry
about the drive and that she was leaving tonight. She
told her she would tell her all about it when she got
there and told her not to worry.

The guy at the U-Haul lot was very nice and made

the process very easy for Lynda. He had it all set up so she could return the hitch to a spot in Cali that he said would be easy to find. He gave Lynda a card with his name and number on it and told her to call if she needed something. She could tell he was staring at her and thought it was because she looked so crazy.

"Hey," he said, "maybe when I'm out that way we could hook up sometime."

Lynda, sighed and said, "Terrence, you're a sweet guy and I really appreciate all of your help. Unfortunately, you've caught me at a crossroad in my life. You see, I'm leaving my husband because I'm a lesbian."

Terrence looked scared and nervous all at the same time. Lynda started laughing out loud. Terrence took it as a sign that she was kidding him.

"Yeah, I've heard that line before," Terrence said. Lynda was walking out the door.

"Call me," Terrence yelled. She waved and never looked back.

When she pulled up to her house she saw something that made her smile. Nikki, Kay, and Renee were all standing there with suitcases. They all had on jeans, T-shirts and tennis shoes. When Lynda got out of the car she just stood there not knowing what to say. They hugged one another, attempting to break the awkward silence that lingered over them.

"Rick is inside," Nikki told Lynda, gesturing toward the house.

The look on Lynda's face clearly said she did not want to see or talk to Rick before she left. She just wasn't ready.

Lynda reluctantly walked into the house and saw Rick standing in the kitchen looking out the window over the sink. He looked lost. When he saw her he stood up straight as if he were actually bracing himself for something.

"Listen, Lynda, I didn't come hear to argue with you, I just came to tell you that I'm sorry for how I did things back there. I really didn't know a proper way to do any of this. I just knew I had to tell you and it seemed like the perfect time when you called and said we should meet. Lynda, I've loved you all of my adolescent and adult life, and I don't think that will ever change. But I realized that I wasn't in love with *us* anymore. I'm not saying it was anyone's fault. It just is what it is," he said, lowering his head.

"Rick, I don't want to talk about this now," Lynda told him with tears in her eyes. "It's too much to digest and I'm way too emotional right now. I just need to take it all in and sort things out logically. Like you said, we've been together a long time, so this is going to take a while to get over. I have some things I need to tell you as well, but they're irrelevant at this point. You've made your decision, and I have to live with it. I'm taking everything that is valuable to me now, so feel free to get rid of anything else you find lying around. I'll call you soon so we can talk about what to do with the house and cars."

"C'mon, Lynda, we can't leave things like this. We have been friends too long. I know I hurt you today, but you apparently had every intention of leaving me today too. What happened to make you come to that decision? Why were you planning on leaving me? Did you somehow find out about T.J.?"

"No. God no! I guess you did me a favor telling me about you and T.J. I'm not really ready to talk about what's going on with me. I promise, once I've sorted things out, we'll have a long talk."

"Lynda, I need to tell you this, though. I know you must have a million questions going through your mind about my sexuality. You must be wondering if I'm gay, if I've always been gay. The answer is no. I didn't realize that I was attracted to men until I went to the escort service."

"Rick, I really don't wanna hear this right now. Really. I can't listen to this." Lynda was so hurt. She felt betrayed. Even though she had had strong feelings for Nikki while she and Rick were married, she never acted on them once they said their vows. She was faithful to Rick and it hurt her to think that he had been unfaithful to her. She couldn't face him. She was confused and angry! She had nothing to say to him. She just wanted to escape to a place where she could come to terms with her life.

"I know, but I didn't want you to leave thinking that you married some kind of freak or something. The truth is I'm attracted to both men and women. I know that now. I didn't know that when we met. I'm still feeling my way through these feelings I have. But it's really important that you know that I have always loved you and that I always will. That's all I wanted to say."

Lynda heard what Rick said and felt a small comfort in knowing that their entire relationship wasn't a lie, but that didn't make things any easier. What was Rick going to say when he found out that she was a lesbian and had been for a long time? She had a lot of soul searching to do before she told Rick. Lynda looked at Rick with tears in her eyes, adjusted her baseball cap, and walked out of the house.

"Ready to go?" Nikki said.

"Yeah," Lynda told them. They all started packing the boxes into the U-Haul and were done in about thirty minutes. The door closed with a loud bang, symbolic of the explosion that seemed to have transformed Lynda's life. Things were changed forever now.

All of the girls had already piled into Lynda's car. Renee glanced over to look at Kay. She wanted desperately to know if Kevin had broken it off with her. From her peripheral vision, Kay could see Renee glaring at her. She wanted desperately to tell Renee that she knew about her and Kevin. Before they could get out of the driveway good, Kay and Renee were already asking Lynda what happened.

"Ladies, we have a three-day drive ahead of us. I promise I will give you every single detail. Even details you don't want to hear."

"Shit, we all probably have some things we need to get off our chest this trip," Kay said, glaring at Renee.

"It's a long ride, we have time," Renee said, looking back at Kay.

"Well, can we stop and get something to eat on the way out? Oh, and I have a bit of news to share with you guys too," Nikki said, smiling.

"Cool, I'm starving," Kay said. "Let's stop at that Waffle Palace over by—"

Lynda stopped the car abruptly.

"*No Waffle Palace!*" she told them.

All the girls looked at each other and shrugged their shoulders. Nikki turned the music all the way up as they turned onto the highway to the sounds of an old-school tune . . . Bob Marley's "No Woman No Cry."

About the Authors

Lisa Nicole Hankerson

Lisa Nicole Hankerson was born in Rochester, New York, but quickly became adept in the Jamaican culture when her parents moved home when she was three years old. It was her move to Detroit, Michigan, however, that brought her to the love of her life, Tony. Tony and Lisa fell in love while attending college at Michigan State University. Since then, they have been married and relocated to Atlanta, Georgia, where they have three handsome boys. *The Key Party* is her first published novel and a testament of her dramatic flare for life and relationships.

Siddeeqah Perryman

Siddeeqah Perryman, originally from Brooklyn, New York, spent her younger years growing up in Atlanta, Georgia. *The Key Party* is her first work as a novelist and fiction writer. Her goal in writing this book was to encourage open-mindedness with respect to relationships. She currently resides in Powder Springs, Georgia, with her daughter, Najeeah, and her son, Nathan.